SIR GAWAIN AND THE GREEN KNIGHT
PEARL AND SIR ORFEO

Sir Gawain
and the
Green Knight

Pearl
AND
Sir Orfeo

TRANSLATED BY J.R.R. TOLKIEN
EDITED BY CHRISTOPHER TOLKIEN

MARINER BOOKS
HOUGHTON MIFFLIN HARCOURT
BOSTON   NEW YORK

First Mariner Books edition 2021

First published in Great Britain by George Allen & Unwin
(Publishers) Ltd 1975

First published by HarperCollins*Publishers* 2021

hmhbooks.com

Library of Congress Cataloging-in-Publication Data is available.
ISBN 978-0-358-65297-7 (pbk.)

Printed in the United States of America
2 2021
4500839341

CONTENTS

PREFACE

When my father, Professor J. R. R. Tolkien, died in 1973
he left unpublished his translations of the medieval
English poems *Sir Gawain and the Green Knight*, *Pearl* and
Sir Orfeo. A form of his *Pearl* translation was in existence
more than thirty years ago, though it was much revised later;
and that of *Sir Gawain* soon after 1950. The latter was broad-
cast on the BBC Third Programme in 1953. His version
of *Sir Orfeo* was also made many years ago, and had been
(I believe) for long laid aside; but he certainly wished to see
it published.

He wished to provide both a general introduction and a
commentary; and it was largely because he could not decide
on the form that these should take that the translations
remained unpublished. On the one hand, he undoubtedly
sought an audience without any knowledge of the original
poems; he wrote of his translation of *Pearl*: 'The Pearl cer-
tainly deserves to be heard by lovers of English poetry who
have not the opportunity or the desire to master its difficult
idiom. To such readers I offer this translation.' But he also
wrote: 'A translation may be a useful form of commentary;
and this version may possibly be acceptable even to those
who already know the original, and possess editions with all
their apparatus.' He wished therefore to explain the basis of

his version in debatable passages; and indeed a very great deal of unshown editorial labour lies behind his translations, which not only reflect his long study of the language and metre of the originals, but were also in some degree the inspiration of it. As he wrote: 'These translations were first made long ago for my own instruction, since a translator must first try to discover as precisely as he can what his original means, and may be led by ever closer attention to understand it better for its own sake. Since I first began I have given to the idiom of these texts very close study, and I have certainly learned more about them than I knew when I first presumed to translate them.'

But the commentary was never written, and the introduction did not get beyond the point of tentative beginnings. My concern in preparing this book has been that it should remain his own; and I have not provided any commentary. Those readers whom he most wished to reach will be content to know that in passages of doubt or difficulty these translations are the product of long scrutiny of the originals, and of great pains to embody his conclusions in a rendering at once precise and metrical; and for explanations and discussions of detail reference must be made to editions of the originals. But readers who are wholly unacquainted with these poems will wish to know something about them; and it seemed to me that if it were at all possible the translations should be introduced in the words of the translator himself, who gave so much time and thought to these works. I have therefore composed the introductory and explanatory parts of the book in the following way.

The first section of the Introduction, on the author of *Sir Gawain* and *Pearl*, is derived from my father's notes. The second section, on *Sir Gawain*, is (in slightly reduced form) a radio talk which he gave after the broadcasts of his translation.

For the third section, the only writing of his on *Pearl* that I could find suitable to the purpose was the original draft for an essay that was subsequently published in revised form. After my father and Professor E.V. Gordon had collaborated in making an edition of *Sir Gawain*, which was published in 1925, they began work on an edition of *Pearl*. In the event, that book was almost entirely the work of Professor Gordon alone, but my father's contribution to it included a small part of the Introduction; and the essay is here reproduced in the form it finally took as the result of their collaboration.* Its appearance here has been made possible through the generosity of Mrs I. L. Gordon. I wish also to thank the Delegates of the Clarendon Press for their permission to use it.

I was not able to discover any writing by my father on the subject of *Sir Orfeo*. Here therefore, in keeping with my general intentions for the book, I have restricted myself to a very brief factual note on the text.

Since a primary object of these translations was the close preservation of the metres of the originals, I thought that the book should contain, for those who want it, an account of the verse-forms of *Sir Gawain* and *Pearl*. The section on *Sir Gawain* is composed from drafts made for, but not used in, the introductory talk to the broadcasts of the translation; and that on the verse-form of *Pearl* from other unpublished notes. There is very little in these accounts (and nothing that is a matter of opinion) that is not in my father's own words.

It is inevitable that in thus using materials written at different times and for different purposes the result should not be entirely homogeneous; but it seemed to me better to accept this consequence than not to use them at all.

---

* *Pearl*, edited by E. V. Gordon, Oxford 1953, pages xi–xix: 'Form and Purpose'.

At his death my father had not finally decided on the form of every line in the translations. In choosing between competing versions I have tried throughout to determine his latest intention, and that has in most cases been discoverable with fair certainty.

Included in this edition is *Sir Gawain and the Green Knight*, the W. P. Ker Memorial Lecture in the University of Glasgow delivered by my father on 15 April 1953. Of this there seems to exist now only one text, a typescript made after the delivery of the lecture (which possibly suggests an intention to publish it), as appears from the statement (p. 124) 'Here the temptation-scenes were read aloud in translation.' My father's translation of *Sir Gawain* into alliterative verse in modern English had then been very recently completed. This translation was broadcast in dramatized form by the BBC in December 1953 (repeated in the following year), and the introduction to the poem which I include here (p. 15) is taken from the radio talk which followed the broadcasts: this, though very brief, is closely related to the lecture printed here.

There are some minor matters concerning its presentation which must be mentioned. Despite my father's statement (p. 111) that 'where quotation is essential I will use a translation which I have just completed', he did not in fact do so throughout, several substantial quotations being given in the original. There does not seem to be any significance in this, however, and I have therefore substituted the translation in such cases. Moreover the translation at that time differed in many details of wording from the revised form published in 1975; and in all such differences I have substituted the latter. I have not inserted the 'temptation scenes' at the point where my father recited them when delivering the lecture, because if these are given in full they run to some 350 lines, and there is no indication in the text of how he reduced them. And lastly, since some readers may wish to refer to the translation rather than to the original poem (edited by J. R. R. Tolkien and E. V. Gordon, second edition revised by N. Davis, Oxford 1967), but the former gives only stanza-numbers and the latter only line-numbers, I have given both: thus 40.970 means that line 970 is found in the 40th stanza.

At the end of the book I have provided a short glossary. On the last page will be found some verses translated by my father from a mediaeval English poem. He called them 'Gawain's Leave-taking', clearly with reference to the passage in *Sir Gawain* where Gawain leaves the castle of Sir Bertilak to go to the tryst at the Green Chapel. The original poem has no connection with *Sir Gawain*; the verses translated are in fact the first three stanzas, and the last, of a somewhat longer poem found among a group of fourteenth-century lyrics with refrains in the Vernon manuscript in the Bodleian Library at Oxford.

Christopher Tolkien

Editor's Note

As Christopher Tolkien notes in his preface, *Sir Gawain and the Green Knight, Pearl and Sir Orfeo* was the very first book by J.R.R. Tolkien edited by him for posthumous publication. Indeed, the editorial work was begun soon after his father's death. Among Christopher's papers is a letter that he wrote to Rayner Unwin, while working on the edition in 1974, where he mentions having come upon the fragment of a wholly different poem translated by his father and entitled by him, 'Gawain's Leave-Taking', and suggests that it might be included, to which Rayner enthusiastically agreed. It is a measure of Christopher's careful stewardship of his father's work that he placed this 'discovery' discreetly at the end of the book, with little explanatory apparatus.

During the preparation of this new edition, Christopher mentioned a remarkable feature present in his father's manuscript of 'Gawain's Leave-Taking' (reproduced as the frontispiece to this edition). Immediately following on from the final stanza there appears a draft of part of the opening Canto of the 'Gest of Beren and Lúthien'. The draft very closely follows the A-text reproduced in *The Lays of Beleriand* (p.157) though precedes it as it contains an alternative couplet after line 12:

> from England unto Eglamar
> o'er folk and field and lands afar.

Christopher noted that evidence that both texts were composed no later than 1929 can be seen by referring to the criticism provided to J.R.R. Tolkien by C.S. Lewis after he read the poem on the night of 6 December 1929, in which Lewis quoted the phrase 'meats were sweet' (*The Lays of Beleriand*, p.315). These words were absent from later versions as Tolkien rewrote the text, very probably as a direct consequence of Lewis's criticism. Christopher concluded that it can therefore be stated with reasonable certainty that J.R.R. Tolkien had *Sir Gawain* in mind even as he worked on the poem that would become *The Lay of Leithian*.

When Christopher and I began work on this new edition, it was intended that Christopher himself would revise his introduction to share the above insight, but was ultimately unable to do so, having laid down his pen for the final time: he died on 16 January 2020. It is fitting that, as we look back upon forty-five years of dedicated service to his father's legacy, and thanks to Christopher's ceaseless love for his father's writings, we may find renewed pleasure and appreciation for the work of J.R.R. Tolkien. And, in 'Gawain's Leave-Taking', a fitting coda to the work of father and son.

'For now at last I take my leave…'

Chris Smith

INTRODUCTION

I

*S*ir *Gawain and the Green Knight* and *Pearl* are both con-
tained in the same unique manuscript, which is now in
the British Museum. Neither poem is given a title. Together
with them are two other poems, also title-less, which are now
known as *Purity* (or *Cleanness*), and *Patience*. All four are in
the same handwriting, which is dated in round figures about
1400; it is small, angular, irregular and often difficult to read,
quite apart from the fading of the ink in the course of time.
But this is the hand of the copyist, not the author. There is
indeed nothing to say that the four poems are the works of
the same poet; but from elaborate comparative study it has
come to be very generally believed that they are.

Of this author, nothing is now known. But he was a major
poet of his day; and it is a solemn thought that his name is
now forgotten, a reminder of the great gaps of ignorance over
which we now weave the thin webs of our literary history. But
something to the purpose may still be learned of this writer
from his works. He was a man of serious and devout mind,
though not without humour; he had an interest in theology,
and some knowledge of it, though an amateur knowledge,
perhaps, rather than a professional; he had Latin and French

and was well enough read in French books, both romantic and instructive; but his home was in the West Midlands of England: so much his language shows, and his metre, and his scenery.

His active life must have lain in the latter half of the fourteenth century, and he was thus a contemporary of Chaucer's; but whereas Chaucer has never become a closed book, and has continued to be read with pleasure since the fifteenth century, *Sir Gawain and the Green Knight* and *Pearl* are practically unintelligible to modern readers. Indeed in their own time the adjectives 'dark' and 'hard' would probably have been applied to these poems by most people who enjoyed the works of Chaucer. For Chaucer was a native of London and the populous South-East of England, and the language which he naturally used has proved to be the foundation of a standard English and literary English of later times; the kind of verse which he composed was the kind which English poets mostly used for the next five hundred years. But the language of this unknown author from the far less populous, far more conservative West Midlands, his grammar, his style, his vocabulary, were in many respects remote from those of London, off the main track of inevitable development; and in *Sir Gawain and the Green Knight* he used the ancient English measure which had descended from antiquity, that kind of verse which is now called 'alliterative'. It aimed at quite different effects from those achieved by the rhymed and syllable-counting metres derived from France and Italy; it seemed harsh and stiff and rugged to those unaccustomed to it. And quite apart from the (from a London point of view) dialectal character of the language, this 'alliterative' verse included in its tradition a number of special verse words, never used in ordinary talk or prose, that were 'dark' to those outside the tradition.

In short, this poet adhered to what is now known as the Alliterative Revival of the fourteenth century, the attempt to use the old native metre and style long rusticated for high and serious writing; and he paid the penalty for its failure, for alliterative verse was not in the event revived. The tides of time, of taste, of language, not to mention political power, trade and wealth, were against it; and all that remains of the chief artist of the 'Revival' is the one manuscript, of which nothing is now known before it found a place in the library of Henry Savile of Bank in Yorkshire, who lived from 1568 to 1617.

And these, then, are the reasons for translation: it is necessary if these poems are not to remain the literary pleasure only of mediaeval specialists. And they are difficult to translate. The main object of the present translations is to preserve the metres, which are essential to the poems as wholes; and to present the language and style, nonetheless, not as they may appear at a superficial glance, archaic, queer, crabbed and rustic, but as they were for the people to whom they were addressed: if English and conservative, yet courtly, wise, and well-bred – educated, indeed learned.

II

Sir Gawain and the Green Knight

If the most certain thing known about the author is that he also wrote *Patience*, *Purity* and *Pearl*, then we have in *Sir Gawain* the work of a man capable of weaving elements taken from diverse sources into a texture of his own; and a man who would have in that labour a serious purpose. I would myself say that it is precisely that purpose that has with its hardness proved the shaping tool which has given form to the material, given it the quality of a good tale on the surface, because it is more than that, if we look closer.

The story is good enough in itself. It is a romance, a fairy-tale for adults, full of life and colour; and it has virtues that would be lost in a summary, though they can be perceived when it is read at length: good scenery, urbane or humorous dialogue, and a skilfully ordered narrative. Of this the most notable example is the long Third Part with its interlacing of the hunting-scenes and the temptations. By this device all three main characters are kept vividly in view during the three crucial days, while the scenes at home and in the field are linked by the Exchange of Winnings, and we watch the gains of the chase diminish as the gains of Sir Gawain increase and the peril of his testing mounts to a crisis.

But all this care in formal construction serves also to make the tale a better vehicle of the 'moral' which the author has imposed on his antique material. He has re-drawn according to his own faith his ideal of knighthood, making it Christian knighthood, showing that the grace and beauty of its courtesy (which he admires) derive from the Divine generosity and grace, Heavenly Courtesy, of which Mary is the supreme creation: the Queen of Courtesy, as he calls her in *Pearl*. This he exhibits symbolically in mathematical perfection in the Pentangle, which he sets on Gawain's shield instead of the heraldic lion or eagle found in other romances. But while in *Pearl* he enlarged his vision of his dead daughter among the blessed to an allegory of the Divine generosity, in *Sir Gawain* he has given life to his ideal by showing it incarnate in a living person, modified by his individual character, so that we can see a man trying to work the ideal out, see its weaknesses (or man's weaknesses).

But he has done more. His major point is the rejection of unchastity and adulterous love, and this was an essential part of the original tradition of *amour courtois* or 'courtly love'; but this he has complicated again, after the way of morals in real life, by involving it in several minor problems of conduct, of courtly behaviour to women and fidelity to men, of what we might call sportsmanship or playing the game. On these problems he has been less explicit, and has left his hearers more or less to form their own views of the scale of their values, and their relation to the governing value of sin and virtue.

So this poem is made to be, as it were, all about Gawain. The rest is a web of circumstance in which he is involved for the revelation of his character and code. The 'Faerie' may with its strangeness and peril enlarge the adventure, making the test more tense and more potent, but Gawain is presented as a credible, living, person; and all that he thinks, or says, or does, is to be seriously considered, as of the real world. His character is drawn so as to make him peculiarly fitted to suffer acutely in the adventure to which he is destined.

We see his almost exaggerated courtesy of speech, his modesty of bearing, which yet goes with a subtle form of pride: a deep sense of his own honour, not to mention, we might say, a pleasure in his own repute as 'this fine father of breeding' (stanza 38). We note also the warmth of his character, generous, even impetuous, which by a slight excess leads him ever to promise more than necessary, beyond the consequences that he can foresee. We are shown his delight in the company of women, his sensitiveness to their beauty, his pleasure in the 'polished play of converse' with them, and at the same time his fervent piety, his devotion to the Blessed Virgin. We see him at the crisis of the action forced to distinguish in scale of value the elements of his code, preserving his chastity, and his loyalty on the highest plane to his host; finally rejecting in fact (if not in empty words) absolute worldly 'courtesy', that is complete obedience to the will of the sovereign lady, rejecting it in favour of virtue.

Yet later we see him, in the last scene with the Green Knight, so overwhelmed by shame at being discovered in a breach of his laughing word, given in a Christmas game, that the honour he has gained in the great test is of small comfort to him. With characteristic excess he vows to wear a badge of disgrace for the rest of his life. In a fit of remorse, so violent that it would be appropriate only to grievous sin, he accuses himself of Greed, Cowardice, and Treachery. Of the first two he is guiltless, except by a casuistry of shame. But how true to life, to a picture of a perhaps not very reflective man of honour, is this shame at being found out (especially at being found out) in something considered rather shabby, whatever in solemn conscience we may think of its real importance. How true also is this equality in emotion aroused by all parts of a personal code of conduct, however various in importance or ultimate sanctions each element may be.

Of the last charge: disloyalty, troth-breach, treachery, all the hard things that he calls it, Gawain was guilty only in so far as he had broken the rules of an absurd game imposed on him by his host (after he had rashly promised to do anything his host asked); and even that was at the request of a lady, made (we may note) after he had accepted her gift, and so was in a cleft stick. Certainly this is an imperfection upon some plane; but on how high a plane, and of what importance? The laughter of the Court of Camelot – and to what higher court in matters of honour could one go? – is probably sufficient answer.

But in terms of literature, undoubtedly this break in the mathematical perfection of an ideal creature, inhuman in flawlessness, is a great improvement. The credibility of Gawain is enormously enhanced by it. He becomes a real man, and we can thus really admire his actual virtue. We can indeed give serious thought to the movements of the English mind in the fourteenth century, which he represents, from which much of our sentiment and ideals of conduct have been derived. We see the attempt to preserve the graces of 'chivalry' and the courtesies, while wedding them, or by wedding them, to Christian morals, to marital fidelity, and indeed married love. The noblest knight of the highest order of Chivalry refuses adultery, places hatred of sin in the last resort above all other motives, and escapes from a temptation that attacks him in the guise of courtesy through grace obtained by prayer. That is what the author of *Sir Gawain and the Green Knight* was mainly thinking about, and with that thought he shaped the poem as we have it.

It was a matter of contemporary concern, for the English. *Sir Gawain* presents in its own way, more explicitly moral and religious, one facet of this movement of thought out of which also grew Chaucer's greatest poem, *Troilus and Criseyde*. Those who read *Sir Gawain* are likely to read the last stanzas of Chaucer's work with a renewed interest.

But if Chaucer's poem is much altered in tone and import from its immediate source in Boccaccio's *Filostrato*, it is utterly removed from the sentiments or ideas in the Homeric Greek poems on the fall of Troy, and still further removed (we may guess) from those of the ancient Aegean world. Research into these things has very little to do with Chaucer. The same is certainly true of *Sir Gawain and the Green Knight*, for which no immediate source has been discovered. For that reason, since I am speaking of this poem and this author, and not of ancient rituals, nor of pagan divinities of the Sun, nor of Fertility, nor of the Dark and the Underworld, in the almost wholly lost antiquity of the North and of these Western Isles – as remote from Sir Gawain of Camelot as the gods of the Aegean are from Troilus and Pandarus in Chaucer – for that reason I have not said anything about the story, or stories, that the author used. Research has discovered a lot about them, especially about the two main themes, the Beheading Challenge and the Test. These are in *Sir Gawain and the Green Knight* cleverly combined, but are elsewhere found separately in varied forms, in Irish or in Welsh or in French. Research of that sort interests men of today greatly; it interests me; but it interested educated men of the fourteenth century very little. They were apt to read poems for what they could get out of them of *sentence*, as they said, of instruction for themselves, and their times; and they were shockingly incurious about authors as persons, or we should have known much more about Geoffrey Chaucer, and the name at least of the author of *Sir Gawain*. But there is not time for everything. Let us be grateful for what we have got, preserved by chary chance: another window of many-coloured glass looking back into the Middle Ages, and giving us another view. Chaucer was a great poet, and by the power of his poetry he tends to dominate the view of his time taken by readers of literature. But his was not the only mood or temper of mind in those days. There were others, such as this author, who while he may have lacked Chaucer's subtlety and flexibility, had, what shall we say? – a nobility to which Chaucer scarcely reached.

III
Editions

Sir Gawain and the Green Knight, edited by J. R. R. Tolkien and E. V. Gordon, Oxford 1925. This has been extensively revised in a second edition by Norman Davis, Oxford 1967.
Pearl, edited by E. V. Gordon, Oxford 1953.
Sir Orfeo, edited by A. J. Bliss, second edition Oxford 1966. This edition contains all three texts of the poem, and a

discussion of the origins of this treatment of the legend of Orpheus and Eurydice.

The Auchinleck text, with the same insertions as are made in the translation, is given in *Fourteenth Century Verse and Prose*, edited by Kenneth Sisam, with a glossary by J. R. R. Tolkien (Oxford University Press).

IV
Note on the text of the translations

The details of presentation (most notably, the absence of line numbers in *Sir Gawain* and *Pearl*, and the use of inverted commas in interior quotations in *Pearl*) are in accordance with my father's wishes.

Line 4 in stanza 42, and line 18 in stanza 98, of the translation of *Sir Gawain* are not in the original. They were introduced into the translation on the assumption that at these points lines had been lost from the original poem, and they are based on suggestions by Sir Israel Gollancz (edition of *Sir Gawain and the Green Knight*, Early English Text Society, 1940).

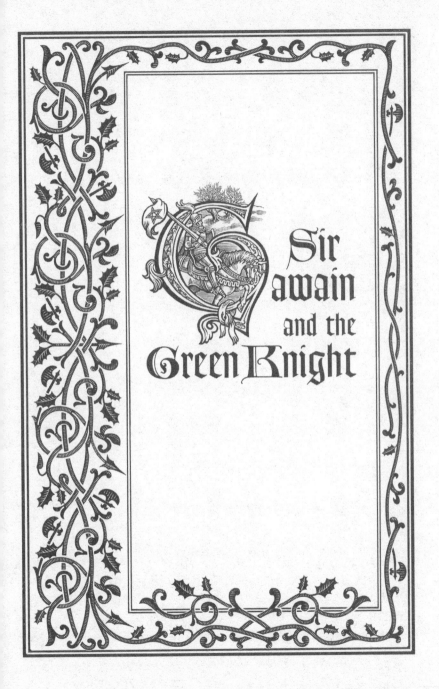

Sir
Gawain
and the
Green Knight

I

WHEN the siege and the assault had ceased at Troy,
and the fortress fell in flame to firebrands and ashes,
the traitor who the contrivance of treason there
fashioned was tried for his treachery, the most true upon
earth – it was Æneas the noble and his renowned kindred
who then laid under them lands, and lords became of
well-nigh all the wealth in the Western Isles. When royal
Romulus to Rome his road had taken, in great pomp and
pride he peopled it first, and named it with his own name
that yet now it bears; Tirius went to Tuscany and towns
founded, Langaberde in Lombardy uplifted halls, and far
over the French flood Felix Brutus on many a broad bank
and brae Britain

establish full fair,
where strange things, strife and sadness,
at whiles in the land did fare,
and each other grief and gladness
oft fast have followed there.

2   And when fair Britain was founded by this famous lord,
bold men were bred there who in battle rejoiced,
and many a time that betid they troubles aroused.
In this domain more marvels have by men been seen
than in any other that I know of since that olden time;
but of all that here abode in Britain as kings
ever was Arthur most honoured, as I have heard men tell.
Wherefore a marvel among men I mean to recall,
a sight strange to see some men have held it,
one of the wildest adventures of the wonders of Arthur.
If you will listen to this lay but a little while now,
I will tell it at once as in town I have heard
      it told,
  as it is fixed and fettered
  in story brave and bold,
  thus linked and truly lettered,
  as was loved in this land of old.

3   This king lay at Camelot at Christmas-tide
with many a lovely lord, lieges most noble,
indeed of the Table Round all those tried brethren,
amid merriment unmatched and mirth without care.
There tourneyed many a time the trusty knights,
and jousted full joyously these gentle lords;
then to the court they came at carols to play.
For there the feast was unfailing full fifteen days,
with all meats and all mirth that men could devise,
such gladness and gaiety as was glorious to hear,
din of voices by day, and dancing by night;
all happiness at the highest in halls and in bowers
had the lords and the ladies, such as they loved most dearly.
With all the bliss of this world they abode together,
the knights most renowned after the name of Christ,

and the ladies most lovely that ever life enjoyed,
and he, king most courteous, who that court possessed.
For all that folk so fair did in their first estate abide,
    Under heaven the first in fame,
    their king most high in pride;
    it would now be hard to name
    a troop in war so tried.

4   While New Year was yet young that yestereve had arrived,
that day double dainties on the dais were served,
when the king was there come with his courtiers to the hall,
and the chanting of the choir in the chapel had ended.
With loud clamour and cries both clerks and laymen
Noel announced anew, and named it full often;
then nobles ran anon with New Year gifts,
Handsels, handsels they shouted, and handed them out,
Competed for those presents in playful debate;
ladies laughed loudly, though they lost the game,
and he that won was not woeful, as may well be believed.
All this merriment they made, till their meat was served;
then they washed, and mannerly went to their seats,
ever the highest for the worthiest, as was held to be best.
Queen Guinevere the gay was with grace in the midst
of the adorned dais set. Dearly was it arrayed:
finest sendal at her sides, a ceiling above her
of true tissue of Tolouse, and tapestries of Tharsia
that were embroidered and bound with the brightest gems
one might prove and appraise to purchase for coin
      any day.
    That loveliest lady there
    on them glanced with eyes of grey;
    that he found ever one more fair
    in sooth might no man say.

5   But Arthur would not eat until all were served;
his youth made him so merry with the moods of a boy,
he liked lighthearted life, so loved he the less
either long to be lying or long to be seated
so worked on him his young blood and wayward brain.
And another rule moreover was his reason besides
that in pride he had appointed: it pleased him not to eat
upon festival so fair, ere he first were apprised
of some strange story or stirring adventure,
or some moving marvel that he might believe in
of noble men, knighthood, or new adventures;
or a challenger should come a champion seeking
to join with him in jousting, in jeopardy to set
his life against life, each allowing the other
the favour of fortune, were she fairer to him.
This was the king's custom, wherever his court was holden,
at each famous feast among his fair company
      in hall
  So his face doth proud appear,
  and he stands up stout and tall,
  all young in the New Year;
  much mirth he makes with all.

6   Thus there stands up straight the stern king himself,
talking before the high table of trifles courtly.
There good Gawain was set at Guinevere's side,
with Agravain a la Dure Main on the other side seated,
both their lord's sister-sons, loyal-hearted knights.
Bishop Baldwin had the honour of the board's service,
and Iwain Urien's son ate beside him.
These dined on the dais and daintily fared,
and many a loyal lord below at the long tables.
Then forth came the first course with fanfare of trumpets,

on which many bright banners bravely were hanging;
noise of drums then anew and the noble pipes,
warbling wild and keen, wakened their music,
so that many hearts rose high hearing their playing.
Then forth was brought a feast, fare of the noblest,
multitude of fresh meats on so many dishes
that free places were few in front of the people
to set the silver things full of soups on cloth
      so white.
  Each lord of his liking there
  without lack took with delight:
  twelve plates to every pair,
  good beer and wine all bright.

7 Now of their service I will say nothing more,
for you are all well aware that no want would there be.
Another noise that was new drew near on a sudden,
so that their lord might have leave at last to take food.
For hardly had the music but a moment ended,
and the first course in the court as was custom been served,
when there passed through the portals a perilous horseman,
the mightiest on middle-earth in measure of height,
from his gorge to his girdle so great and so square,
and his loins and his limbs so long and so huge,
that half a troll upon earth I trow that he was,
but the largest man alive at least I declare him;
and yet the seemliest for his size that could sit on a horse,
for though in back and in breast his body was grim,
both his paunch and his waist were properly slight,
and all his features followed his fashion so gay
      in mode;
  for at the hue men gaped aghast
  in his face and form that showed;

as a fay-man fell he passed,
and green all over glowed.

8 All of green were they made, both garments and man:
a coat tight and close that clung to his sides;
a rich robe above it all arrayed within
with fur finely trimmed, shewing fair fringes
of handsome ermine gay, as his hood was also,
that was lifted from his locks and laid on his shoulders;
and trim hose tight-drawn of tincture alike
that clung to his calves; and clear spurs below
of bright gold on silk broideries banded most richly,
though unshod were his shanks, for shoeless he rode.
And verily all this vesture was of verdure clear,
both the bars on his belt, and bright stones besides
that were richly arranged in his array so fair,
set on himself and on his saddle upon silk fabrics:
it would be too hard to rehearse one half of the trifles
that were embroidered upon them, what with birds and
                                              with flies
in a gay glory of green, and ever gold in the midst.
The pendants of his poitrel, his proud crupper,
his molains, and all the metal to say more, were enamelled,
even the stirrups that he stood in were stained of the same;
and his saddlebows in suit, and their sumptuous skirts,
which ever glimmered and glinted all with green jewels;
even the horse that upheld him in hue was the same,
          I tell:
     a green horse great and thick,
     a stallion stiff to quell,
     in broidered bridle quick:
     he matched his master well.

9   Very gay was this great man guised all in green,
and the hair of his head with his horse's accorded:
fair flapping locks enfolding his shoulders,
a big beard like a bush over his breast hanging
that with the handsome hair from his head falling
was sharp shorn to an edge just short of his elbows,
so that half his arms under it were hid, as it were
in a king's capadoce that encloses his neck.
The mane of that mighty horse was of much the same sort,
well curled and all combed, with many curious knots
woven in with gold wire about the wondrous green,
ever a strand of the hair and a string of the gold;
the tail and the top-lock were twined all to match
and both bound with a band of a brilliant green:
with dear jewels bedight to the dock's ending,
and twisted then on top was a tight-knitted knot
on which many burnished bells of bright gold jingled.
Such a mount on middle-earth, or man to ride him,
was never beheld in that hall with eyes ere that time;
     for there
  his glance was as lightning bright,
  so did all that saw him swear;
  no man would have the might,
  they thought, his blows to bear.

10 And yet he had not a helm, nor a hauberk either,
not a pisane, not a plate that was proper to arms;
not a shield, not a shaft, for shock or for blow,
but in his one hand he held a holly-bundle,
that is greatest in greenery when groves are leafless,
and an axe in the other, ugly and monstrous,
a ruthless weapon aright for one in rhyme to describe:
the head was as large and as long as an ellwand,

a branch of green steel and of beaten gold;
the bit, burnished bright and broad at the edge,
as well shaped for shearing as sharp razors;
the stem was a stout staff, by which sternly he gripped it,
all bound with iron about to the base of the handle,
and engraven in green in graceful patterns,
lapped round with a lanyard that was lashed to the head
and down the length of the haft was looped many times;
and tassels of price were tied there in plenty
to bosses of the bright green, braided most richly.
Such was he that now hastened in, the hall entering,
pressing forward to the dais – no peril he feared.
To none gave he greeting, gazing above them,
and the first word that he winged: 'Now where is', he said,
'the governor of this gathering? For gladly I would
on the same set my sight, and with himself now talk
   in town.'
  On the courtiers he cast his eye,
   and rolled it up and down;
  he stopped, and stared to espy
   who there had most renown.

11 Then they looked for a long while, on that lord gazing;
for every man marvelled what it could mean indeed
that horseman and horse such a hue should come by
as to grow green as the grass, and greener it seemed,
than green enamel on gold glowing far brighter.
All stared that stood there and stole up nearer,
watching him and wondering what in the world he
         would do.
For many marvels they had seen, but to match this nothing;
wherefore a phantom and fay-magic folk there thought it,
and so to answer little eager was any of those knights,

and astounded at his stern voice stone-still they sat there
in a swooning silence through that solemn chamber,
as if all had dropped into a dream, so died their voices
   away.
  Not only, I deem, for dread;
  but of some 'twas their courtly way
  to allow their lord and head
  to the guest his word to say.

12 Then Arthur before the high dais beheld this wonder,
and freely with fair words, for fearless was he ever,
saluted him, saying: 'Lord, to this lodging thou'rt welcome!
The head of this household Arthur my name is.
Alight, as thou lovest me, and linger, I pray thee;
and what may thy wish be in a while we shall learn.'
'Nay, so help me,' quoth the horseman, 'He that on high
          is throned,
to pass any time in this place was no part of my errand.
But since thy praises, prince, so proud are uplifted,
and thy castle and courtiers are accounted the best,
the stoutest in steel-gear that on steeds may ride,
most eager and honourable of the earth's people,
valiant to vie with in other virtuous sports,
and here is knighthood renowned, as is noised in my ears:
'tis that has fetched me hither, by my faith, at this time.
You may believe by this branch that I am bearing here
that I pass as one in peace, no peril seeking.
For had I set forth to fight in fashion of war,
I have a hauberk at home, and a helm also,
a shield, and a sharp spear shining brightly,
and other weapons to wield too, as well I believe;
but since I crave for no combat, my clothes are softer.
Yet if thou be so bold, as abroad is published,

33

thou wilt grant of thy goodness the game that I ask for
    by right.'
Then Arthur answered there,
and said: 'Sir, noble knight,
if battle thou seek thus bare,
thou'lt fail not here to fight.'

13   'Nay, I wish for no warfare, on my word I tell thee!
Here about on these benches are but beardless children.
Were I hasped in armour on a high charger,
there is no man here to match me – their might is so feeble.
And so I crave in this court only a Christmas pastime,
since it is Yule and New Year, and you are young here and
                                       merry.
If any so hardy in this house here holds that he is,
if so bold be his blood or his brain be so wild,
that he stoutly dare strike one stroke for another,
then I will give him as my gift this guisarm costly,
this axe – 'tis heavy enough – to handle as he pleases;
and I will abide the first brunt, here bare as I sit.
If any fellow be so fierce as my faith to test,
hither let him haste to me and lay hold of this weapon –
I hand it over for ever, he can have it as his own –
and I will stand a stroke from him, stock-still on this floor,
provided thou'lt lay down this law: that I may deliver
him another.
      Claim I!
And yet a respite I'll allow,
till a year and a day go by.
Come quick, and let's see now
if any here dare reply!'

14 If he astounded them at first, yet stiller were then
    all the household in the hall, both high men and low.
    The man on his mount moved in his saddle,
    and rudely his red eyes he rolled then about,
    bent his bristling brows all brilliantly green,
    and swept round his beard to see who would rise.
    When none in converse would accost him, he coughed
                                      then loudly,
    stretched himself haughtily and straightway exclaimed:
    'What! Is this Arthur's house,' said he thereupon,
    'the rumour of which runs through realms unnumbered?
    Where now is your haughtiness, and your high conquests,
    your fierceness and fell mood, and your fine boasting?
    Now are the revels and the royalty of the Round Table
    overwhelmed by a word by one man spoken,
    for all blench now abashed ere a blow is offered!'
    With that he laughed so loud that their lord was angered,
    the blood shot for shame into his shining cheeks
            and face;
        as wroth as wind he grew,
        so all did in that place.
        Then near to the stout man drew
        the king of fearless race,

15 And said: 'Marry! Good man, 'tis madness thou askest,
    and since folly thou hast sought, thou deservest to find it.
    I know no lord that is alarmed by thy loud words here.
    Give me now thy guisarm, in God's name, sir,
    and I will bring thee the blessing thou hast begged to
                                      receive.'
    Quick then he came to him and caught it from his hand.
    Then the lordly man loftily alighted on foot.
    Now Arthur holds his axe, and the haft grasping

35

sternly he stirs it about, his stroke considering.
The stout man before him there stood his full height,
higher than any in that house by a head and yet more.
With stern face as he stood he stroked at his beard,
and with expression impassive he pulled down his coat,
no more disturbed or distressed at the strength of his blows
than if someone as he sat had served him a drink
     of wine.
    From beside the queen Gawain
    to the king did then incline:
    'I implore with prayer plain
    that this match should now be mine.'

16 'Would you, my worthy lord,' said Wawain to the king,
    'bid me abandon this bench and stand by you there,
    so that I without discourtesy might be excused from the
                                           table,
    and my liege lady were not loth to permit me,
    I would come to your counsel before your courtiers fair.
    For I find it unfitting, as in fact it is held,
    when a challenge in your chamber makes choice so exalted,
    though you yourself be desirous to accept it in person,
    while many bold men about you on bench are seated:
    on earth there are, I hold, none more honest of purpose,
    no figures fairer on field where fighting is waged.
    I am the weakest, I am aware, and in wit feeblest,
    and the least loss, if I live not, if one would learn the truth.
    Only because you are my uncle is honour given me:
    save your blood in my body I boast of no virtue;
    and since this affair is so foolish that it nowise befits you,
    and I have requested it first, accord it then to me!
    If my claim is uncalled-for without cavil shall judge
        this court.'

To consult the knights draw near,
and this plan they all support;
the king with crown to clear,
and give Gawain the sport.

17 The king then commanded that he quickly should rise,
and he readily uprose and directly approached,
kneeling humbly before his highness, and laying hand on
                                     the weapon;
and he lovingly relinquished it, and lifting his hand
gave him God's blessing, and graciously enjoined him
that his hand and his heart should be hardy alike.
'Take care, cousin,' quoth the king, 'one cut to address,
and if thou learnest him his lesson, I believe very well
that thou wilt bear any blow that he gives back later.'
Gawain goes to the great man with guisarm in hand,
and he boldly abides there – he blenched not at all.
Then next said to Gawain the knight all in green:
'Let's tell again our agreement, ere we go any further.
I'd know first, sir knight, thy name; I entreat thee
to tell it me truly, that I may trust in thy word.'
'In good faith,' quoth the good knight, 'I Gawain am called
who bring thee this buffet, let be what may follow;
and at this time a twelvemonth in thy turn have another
with whatever weapon thou wilt, and in the world with
      none else but me.'
  The other man answered again:
  'I am passing pleased,' said he,
  'upon my life, Sir Gawain,
that this stroke should be struck by thee.'

18 'Begad,' said the green knight, 'Sir Gawain, I am pleased
to find from thy fist the favour I asked for!

And thou hast promptly repeated and plainly hast stated
without abatement the bargain I begged of the king here;
save that thou must assure me, sir, on thy honour
that thou'lt seek me thyself, search where thou thinkest
I may be found near or far, and fetch thee such payment
as thou deliverest me today before these lordly people.'
'Where should I light on thee,' quoth Gawain, 'where look
                        for thy place?
I have never learned where thou livest, by the Lord that
                        made me,
and I know thee not, knight, thy name nor thy court.
But teach me the true way, and tell what men call thee,
and I will apply all my purpose the path to discover:
and that I swear thee for certain and solemnly promise.'
'That is enough in New Year, there is need of no more!'
said the great man in green to Gawain the courtly.
'If I tell thee the truth of it, when I have taken the knock,
and thou handily hast hit me, if in haste I announce then
my house and my home and mine own title,
then thou canst call and enquire and keep the agreement;
and if I waste not a word, thou'lt win better fortune,
for thou mayst linger in thy land and look no further –
     but stay!
    To thy grim tool now take heed, sir!
    Let us try thy knocks today!'
    'Gladly', said he, 'indeed, sir!'
    and his axe he stroked in play.

19 The Green Knight on the ground now gets himself ready,
leaning a little with the head he lays bare the flesh,
and his locks long and lovely he lifts over his crown,
letting the naked neck as was needed appear.
His left foot on the floor before him placing,

Gawain gripped on his axe, gathered and raised it,
from aloft let it swiftly land where 'twas naked,
so that the sharp of his blade shivered the bones,
and sank clean through the clear fat and clove it asunder,
and the blade of the bright steel then bit into the ground.
The fair head to the floor fell from the shoulders,
and folk fended it with their feet as forth it went rolling;
the blood burst from the body, bright on the greenness,
and yet neither faltered nor fell the fierce man at all,
but stoutly he strode forth, still strong on his shanks,
and roughly he reached out among the rows that stood
                                                    there,
caught up his comely head and quickly upraised it,
and then hastened to his horse, laid hold of the bridle,
stepped into stirrup-iron, and strode up aloft,
his head by the hair in his hand holding;
and he settled himself then in the saddle as firmly
as if unharmed by mishap, though in the hall he might
        wear no head.
    His trunk he twisted round,
    that gruesome body that bled,
    and many fear then found,
    as soon as his speech was sped.

20 For the head in his hand he held it up straight,
    towards the fairest at the table he twisted the face,
    and it lifted up its eyelids and looked at them broadly,
    and made such words with its mouth as may be recounted.
    'See thou get ready, Gawain, to go as thou vowedst,
    and as faithfully seek till thou find me, good sir,
    as thou hast promised in this place in the presence of
                                                    these knights.
    To the Green Chapel go thou, and get thee, I charge thee,

such a dint as thou hast dealt – indeed thou hast earned
a nimble knock in return on New Year's morning!
The Knight of the Green Chapel I am known to many,
so if to find me thou endeavour, thou'lt fail not to do so.
Therefore come! Or to be called a craven thou deservest.'
With a rude roar and rush his reins he turned then,
and hastened out through the hall-door with his head in
                                          his hand,
and fire of the flint flew from the feet of his charger.
To what country he came in that court no man knew,
no more than they had learned from what land he had
                                          journeyed.

      Meanwhile,
  the king and Sir Gawain
  at the Green Man laugh and smile;
  yet to men had appeared, 'twas plain,
  a marvel beyond denial.

21 Though Arthur the high king in his heart marvelled,
he let no sign of it be seen, but said then aloud
to the queen so comely with courteous words:
'Dear Lady, today be not downcast at all!
Such cunning play well becomes the Christmas tide,
interludes, and the like, and laughter and singing,
amid these noble dances of knights and of dames.
Nonetheless to my food I may fairly betake me,
for a marvel I have met, and I may not deny it.'
He glanced at Sir Gawain and with good point he said:
'Come, hang up thine axe, sir! It has hewn now enough.'
And over the table they hung it on the tapestry behind,
where all men might remark it, a marvel to see,
and by its true token might tell of that adventure.
Then to a table they turned, those two lords together,

the king and his good kinsman, and courtly men served them
with all dainties double, the dearest there might be,
with all manner of meats and with minstrelsy too.
With delight that day they led, till to the land came the
      night again.
  Sir Gawain, now take heed
  lest fear make thee refrain
  from daring the dangerous deed
  that thou in hand hast ta'en!

II

WITH this earnest of high deeds thus Arthur began the
young year, for brave vows he yearned to hear made.
Though such words were wanting when they went to
table, now of fell work to full grasp filled were their hands.
Gawain was gay as he began those games in the hall, but if
the end be unhappy, hold it no wonder! For though men
be merry of mood when they have mightily drunk, a year
slips by swiftly, never the same returning; the outset to the
ending is equal but seldom. And so this Yule passed over
and the year after, and severally the seasons ensued in their
turn: after Christmas there came the crabbed Lenten that
with fish tries the flesh and with food more meagre; but
then the weather in the world makes war on the winter,
cold creeps into the earth, clouds are uplifted, shining
rain is shed in showers that all warm fall on the fair turf,
flowers there open, of grounds and of groves green is the
raiment, birds are busy a-building and bravely are singing
for sweetness of the soft summer that will soon be on
      the way;
  and blossoms burgeon and blow

41

in hedgerows bright and gay;
then glorious musics go
through the woods in proud array.

23 After the season of summer with its soft breezes,
when Zephyr goes sighing through seeds and herbs,
right glad is the grass that grows in the open,
when the damp dewdrops are dripping from the leaves
to greet a gay glance of the glistening sun.
But then Harvest hurries in, and hardens it quickly,
warns it before winter to wax to ripeness.
He drives with his drought the dust, till it rises
from the face of the land and flies up aloft;
wild wind in the welkin makes war on the sun,
the leaves loosed from the linden alight on the ground,
and all grey is the grass that green was before:
all things ripen and rot that rose up at first,
and so the year runs away in yesterdays many,
and here winter wends again, as by the way of the world
          it ought,
    until the Michaelmas moon
    has winter's boding brought;
    Sir Gawain then full soon
    of his grievous journey thought.

24 And yet till All Hallows with Arthur he lingered,
who furnished on that festival a feast for the knight
with much royal revelry of the Round Table.
The knights of renown and noble ladies
all for the love of that lord had longing at heart,
but nevertheless the more lightly of laughter they spoke:
many were joyless who jested for his gentle sake.
For after their meal mournfully he reminded his uncle

that his departure was near, and plainly he said:
'Now liege-lord of my life, for leave I beg you.
You know the quest and the compact; I care not further
to trouble you with tale of it, save a trifling point:
I must set forth to my fate without fail in the morning,
as God will me guide, the Green Man to seek.'
Those most accounted in the castle came then together,
Iwain and Erric and others not a few,
Sir Doddinel le Savage, the Duke of Clarence,
Lancelot, and Lionel, and Lucan the Good,
Sir Bors and Sir Bedivere that were both men of might,
and many others of mark with Mador de la Porte.
All this company of the court the king now approached
to comfort the knight with care in their hearts.
Much mournful lament was made in the hall
that one so worthy as Wawain should wend on that errand,
To endure a deadly dint and deal no more
      with blade.
   The knight ever made good cheer,
   saying, 'Why should I be dismayed?
   Of doom the fair or drear
   by a man must be assayed.'

25 He remained there that day, and in the morning got ready,
asked early for his arms, and they all were brought him.
First a carpet of red silk was arrayed on the floor,
and the gilded gear in plenty there glittered upon it.
The stern man stepped thereon and the steel things
                        handled,
dressed in a doublet of damask of Tharsia,
and over it a cunning capadoce that was closed at the throat
and with fair ermine was furred all within.
Then sabatons first they set on his feet,

his legs lapped in steel in his lordly greaves,
on which the polains they placed, polished and shining
and knit upon his knees with knots all of gold;
then the comely cuisses that cunningly clasped
the thick thews of his thighs they with thongs on him tied;
and next the byrnie, woven of bright steel rings
upon costly quilting, enclosed him about;
and armlets well burnished upon both of his arms,
with gay elbow-pieces and gloves of plate,
and all the goodly gear to guard him whatever
       betide;
   coat-armour richly made,
   gold spurs on heel in pride;
   girt with a trusty blade,
   silk belt about his side.

26 When he was hasped in his armour his harness was splendid:
the least latchet or loop was all lit with gold.
Thus harnessed as he was he heard now his Mass,
that was offered and honoured at the high altar;
and then he came to the king and his court-companions,
and with love he took leave of lords and of ladies;
and they kissed him and escorted him, and to Christ him
       commended.
And now Gringolet stood groomed, and girt with a saddle
gleaming right gaily with many gold fringes,
and all newly for the nonce nailed at all points;
adorned with bars was the bridle, with bright gold banded;
the apparelling proud of poitrel and of skirts,
and the crupper and caparison accorded with the
       saddlebows:
all was arrayed in red with rich gold studded,
so that it glittered and glinted as a gleam of the sun.

Then he in hand took the helm and in haste kissed it:
strongly was it stapled and stuffed within;
it sat high upon his head and was hasped at the back,
and a light kerchief was laid o'er the beaver,
all braided and bound with the brightest gems
upon broad silken broidery, with birds on the seams
like popinjays depainted, here preening and there,
turtles and true-loves, entwined as thickly
as if many sempstresses had the sewing full seven winters
     in hand.
   A circlet of greater price
   his crown about did band;
   The diamonds point-device
   there blazing bright did stand.

27   Then they brought him his blazon that was of brilliant gules
with the pentangle depicted in pure hue of gold.
By the baldric he caught it and about his neck cast it:
right well and worthily it went with the knight.
And why the pentangle is proper to that prince so noble
I intend now to tell you, though it may tarry my story.
It is a sign that Solomon once set on a time
to betoken Troth, as it is entitled to do;
for it is a figure that in it five points holdeth,
and each line overlaps and is linked with another,
and every way it is endless; and the English, I hear,
everywhere name it the Endless Knot.
So it suits well this knight and his unsullied arms;
for ever faithful in five points, and five times under each,
Gawain as good was acknowledged and as gold refinéd,
devoid of every vice and with virtues adorned.
     So there
   the pentangle painted new

he on shield and coat did wear,
as one of word most true
and knight of bearing fair.

28 First faultless was he found in his five senses,
and next in his five fingers he failed at no time,
and firmly on the Five Wounds all his faith was set
that Christ received on the cross, as the Creed tells us;
and wherever the brave man into battle was come,
on this beyond all things was his earnest thought:
that ever from the Five Joys all his valour he gained
that to Heaven's courteous Queen once came from her

Child.

For which cause the knight had in comely wise
on the inner side of his shield her image depainted,
that when he cast his eyes thither his courage never failed.
The fifth five that was used, as I find, by this knight
was free-giving and friendliness first before all,
and chastity and chivalry ever changeless and straight,
and piety surpassing all points: these perfect five
were hasped upon him harder than on any man else.
Now these five series, in sooth, were fastened on this knight,
and each was knit with another and had no ending,
but were fixed at five points that failed not at all,
coincided in no line nor sundered either,
not ending in any angle anywhere, as I discover,
wherever the process was put in play or passed to an end.
Therefore on his shining shield was shaped now this knot,
royally with red gules upon red gold set:
this is the pure pentangle as people of learning
        have taught.
    Now Gawain in brave array
    his lance at last hath caught.

He gave them all good day,
for evermore as he thought.

29 He spurned his steed with the spurs and sprang on his way
so fiercely that the flint-sparks flashed out behind him.
All who beheld him so honourable in their hearts were
                    sighing,
and assenting in sooth one said to another,
grieving for that good man: 'Before God, 'tis a shame
that thou, lord, must be lost, who art in life so noble!
To meet his match among men, Marry, 'tis not easy!
To behave with more heed would have behoved one of
                    sense,
and that dear lord duly a duke to have made,
illustrious leader of liegemen in this land as befits him;
and that would better have been than to be butchered to
                    death,
beheaded by an elvish man for an arrogant vaunt.
Who can recall any king that such a course ever took
as knights quibbling at court at their Christmas games!'
Many warm tears outwelling there watered their eyes,
when that lord so beloved left the castle
      that day.
  No longer he abode,
  but swiftly went his way;
  bewildering ways he rode,
  as the book I heard doth say.

30 Now he rides thus arrayed through the realm of Logres,
Sir Gawain in God's care, though no game now he found it.
Oft forlorn and alone he lodged of a night
where he found not afforded him such fare as pleased him.
He had no friend but his horse in the forests and hills,

no man on his march to commune with but God,
till anon he drew near unto Northern Wales.
All the isles of Anglesey he held on his left,
and over the fords he fared by the flats near the sea,
and then over by the Holy Head to high land again
in the wilderness of Wirral: there wandered but few
who with goodwill regarded either God or mortal.
And ever he asked as he went on of all whom he met
if they had heard any news of a knight that was green
in any ground thereabouts, or of the Green Chapel.
And all denied it, saying nay, and that never in their lives
a single man had they seen that of such a colour
        could be.
    The knight took pathways strange
    by many a lonesome lea,
    and oft his view did change
    that chapel ere he could see.

31 Many a cliff he climbed o'er in countries unknown,
    far fled from his friends without fellowship he rode.
    At every wading or water on the way that he passed
    he found a foe before him, save at few for a wonder;
    and so foul were they and fell that fight he must needs.
    So many a marvel in the mountains he met in those lands
    that 'twould be tedious the tenth part to tell you thereof.
    At whiles with worms he wars, and with wolves also,
    at whiles with wood-trolls that wandered in the crags,
    and with bulls and with bears and boars, too, at times;
    and with ogres that hounded him from the heights of the

                                                    fells.

    Had he not been stalwart and staunch and steadfast in God,
    he doubtless would have died and death had met often;
    for though war wearied him much, the winter was worse,

when the cold clear water from the clouds spilling
froze ere it had fallen upon the faded earth.
Wellnigh slain by the sleet he slept ironclad
more nights than enow in the naked rocks,
where clattering from the crest the cold brook tumbled,
and hung high o'er his head in hard icicles.
Thus in peril and pain and in passes grievous
till Christmas-eve that country he crossed all alone
      in need.
   The knight did at that tide
   his plaint to Mary plead,
   her rider's road to guide
   and to some lodging lead.

32 By a mount in the morning merrily he was riding
into a forest that was deep and fearsomely wild,
with high hills at each hand, and hoar woods beneath
of huge aged oaks by the hundred together;
the hazel and the hawthorn were huddled and tangled
with rough ragged moss around them trailing,
with many birds bleakly on the bare twigs sitting
that piteously piped there for pain of the cold.
The good man on Gringolet goes now beneath them
through many marshes and mires, a man all alone,
troubled lest a truant at that time he should prove
from the service of the sweet Lord, who on that selfsame
                           night
of a maid became man our mourning to conquer.
And therefore sighing he said: 'I beseech thee, O Lord,
and Mary, who is the mildest mother most dear,
for some harbour where with honour I might hear the Mass
and thy Matins tomorrow. This meekly I ask,
and thereto promptly I pray with Pater and Ave

and Creed.'
    In prayer he now did ride,
    lamenting his misdeed;
    he blessed him oft and cried,
    'The Cross of Christ me speed!'

33 The sign on himself he had set but thrice,
ere a mansion he marked within a moat in the forest,
on a low mound above a lawn, laced under the branches
of many a burly bole round about by the ditches:
the castle most comely that ever a king possessed
placed amid a pleasance with a park all about it,
within a palisade of pointed pales set closely
that took its turn round the trees for two miles or more.
Gawain from the one side gazed on the stronghold
as it shimmered and shone through the shining oaks,
and then humbly he doffed his helm, and with honour he
                                           thanked
Jesus and Saint Julian, who generous are both,
who had courtesy accorded him and to his cry harkened.
'Now bon hostel,' quoth the knight, 'I beg of you still!'
Then he goaded Gringolet with his gilded heels,
and he chose by good chance the chief pathway
and brought his master bravely to the bridge's end
    at last.
    That brave bridge was up-hauled,
    the gates were bolted fast;
    the castle was strongly walled,
    it feared no wind or blast.

34 Then he stayed his steed that on the steep bank halted
above the deep double ditch that was drawn round the place.

The wall waded in the water wondrous deeply,
and up again to a huge height in the air it mounted,
all of hard hewn stone to the high cornice,
fortified under the battlement in the best fashion
and topped with fair turrets set by turns about
that had many graceful loopholes with a good outlook:
that knight a better barbican had never seen built.
And inwards he beheld the hall uprising,
tall towers set in turns, and as tines clustering
the fair finials, joined featly, so fine and so long,
their capstones all carven with cunning and skill.
Many chalk-white chimneys he chanced to espy
upon the roofs of towers all radiant white;
so many a painted pinnacle was peppered about,
among the crenelles of the castle clustered so thickly
that all pared out of paper it appeared to have been.
The gallant knight on his great horse good enough
                                 thought it,
if he could come by any course that enclosure to enter,
to harbour in that hostel while the holy day lasted
      with delight.
   He called, and there came with speed
   a porter blithe and bright;
   on the wall he learned his need,
   and hailed the errant knight.

35 'Good sir', quoth Gawain, 'will you go with my message
to the high lord of this house for harbour to pray?'
'Yes, by Peter!' quoth the porter, 'and I promise indeed
that you will, sir, be welcome while you wish to stay here.'
Then quickly the man went and came again soon,
servants bringing civilly to receive there the knight.

They drew down the great drawbridge, and duly came
                                                    forth,
and on the cold earth on their knees in courtesy knelt
to welcome this wayfarer with such worship as they knew.
They delivered him the broad gates and laid them wide
                                                    open,
and he readily bade them rise and rode o'er the bridge.
Several servants then seized the saddle as he alighted,
and many stout men his steed to a stable then led,
while knights and esquires anon descended
to guide there in gladness this guest to the hall.
When he raised up his helm many ran there in haste
to have it from his hand, his highness to serve;
his blade and his blazon both they took charge of.
Then he greeted graciously those good men all,
and many were proud to approach him, that prince to
                                                    honour.

All hasped in his harness to hall they brought him,
where a fair blaze in the fireplace fiercely was burning.
Then the lord of that land leaving his chamber
came mannerly to meet the man on the floor.
He said: 'You are welcome at your wish to dwell here.
What is here, all is your own, to have in your rule
        and sway.'
    'Gramercy!' quoth Gawain,
    'May Christ you this repay!'
    As men that to meet were fain
    they both embraced that day.

36 Gawain gazed at the good man who had greeted him kindly,
    and he thought bold and big was the baron of the castle,
    very large and long, and his life at the prime:
    broad and bright was his beard, and all beaver-hued,

stern, strong in his stance upon stalwart legs,
his face fell as fire, and frank in his speech;
and well it suited him, in sooth, as it seemed to the knight,
a lordship to lead untroubled over lieges trusty.
To a chamber the lord drew him, and charged men at once
to assign him an esquire to serve and obey him;
and there to wait on his word many worthy men were,
who brought him to a bright bower where the bedding was
                                        splendid:
there were curtains of costly silk with clear-golden hems,
and coverlets cunning-wrought with quilts most lovely
of bright ermine above, embroidered at the sides,
hangings running on ropes with red-gold rings,
carpets of costly damask that covered the walls
and the floor under foot fairly to match them.
There they despoiled him, speaking to him gaily,
his byrnie doing off and his bright armour.
Rich robes then readily men ran to bring him,
for him to change, and to clothe him, having chosen the
                                        best.

As soon as he had donned one and dressed was therein,
as it sat on him seemly with its sailing skirts,
then verily in his visage a vision of Spring
to each man there appeared, and in marvellous hues
bright and beautiful was all his body beneath.
That knight more noble was never made by Christ
        they thought.
    He came none knew from where,
    but it seemed to them he ought
    to be a prince beyond compare
    in the field where fell men fought.

37 A chair before the chimney where charcoal was burning
was made ready in his room, all arrayed and covered
with cushions upon quilted cloths that were cunningly
                                                    made.

Then a comely cloak was cast about him
of bright silk brocade, embroidered most richly
and furred fairly within with fells of the choicest
and all edged with ermine, and its hood was to match;
and he sat in that seat seemly and noble
and warmed himself with a will, and then his woes were
                                                    amended.

Soon up on good trestles a table was raised
and clad with a clean cloth clear white to look on;
there was surnape, salt-cellar, and silvern spoons.
He then washed as he would and went to his food,
and many worthy men with worship waited upon him;
soups they served of many sorts, seasoned most choicely,
in double helpings, as was due, and divers sorts of fish;
some baked in bread, some broiled on the coals,
some seethed, some in gravy savoured with spices,
and all with condiments so cunning that it caused him
                                                    delight.

A fair feast he called it frankly and often,
graciously, when all the good men together there pressed
                                                    him:

'Now pray,
this penance deign to take;
'twill improve another day!'
The man much mirth did make,
for wine to his head made way.

38 Then inquiry and question were carefully put
touching personal points to that prince himself,

till he courteously declared that to the court he belonged
that high Arthur in honour held in his sway,
who was the right royal King of the Round Table,
and 'twas Gawain himself that as their guest now sat
and had come for that Christmas, as the case had turned

out.

When the lord had learned whom luck had brought him,
loud laughed he thereat, so delighted he was,
and they made very merry, all the men in that castle,
and to appear in the presence were pressing and eager
of one who all profit and prowess and perfect manners
comprised in his person, and praise ever gained;
of all men on middle-earth he most was admired.
Softly each said then in secret to his friend:
'Now fairly shall we mark the fine points of manners,
and the perfect expressions of polished converse.
How speech is well spent will be expounded unasked,
since we have found here this fine father of breeding.
God has given us of His goodness His grace now indeed,
Who such a guest as Gawain has granted us to have!
When blissful men at board for His birth sing blithe
        at heart,
    what manners high may mean
    this knight will now impart.
    Who hears him will, I ween
    of love-speech learn some art.'

39 When his dinner was done and he duly had risen,
    it now to the night-time very near had drawn.
    The chaplains then took to the chapel their way
    and rang the bells richly, as rightly they should,
    for the solemn evensong of the high season.
    The lord leads the way, and his lady with him;

55

into a goodly oratory gracefully she enters.
Gawain follows gladly, and goes there at once
and the lord seizes him by the sleeve and to a seat leads him,
kindly acknowledges him and calls him by his name,
saying that most welcome he was of all guests in the world.
And he grateful thanks gave him, and each greeted the
                                                          other,
and they sat together soberly while the service lasted.
Then the lady longed to look at this knight;
and from her closet she came with many comely maidens.
She was fairer in face, in her flesh and her skin,
her proportions, her complexion, and her port than all
                                                          others,
and more lovely than Guinevere to Gawain she looked.
He came through the chancel to pay court to her grace;
leading her by the left hand another lady was there
who was older than she, indeed ancient she seemed,
and held in high honour by all men about her.
But unlike in their looks those ladies appeared,
for if the younger was youthful, yellow was the elder;
with rose-hue the one face was richly mantled,
rough wrinkled cheeks rolled on the other;
on the kerchiefs of the one many clear pearls were,
her breast and bright throat were bare displayed,
fairer than white snow that falls on the hills;
the other was clad with a cloth that enclosed all her neck,
enveloped was her black chin with chalk-white veils,
her forehead folded in silk, and so fumbled all up,
so topped up and trinketed and with trifles bedecked
that naught was bare of that beldame but her brows all
                                                          black,
her two eyes and her nose and her naked lips,
and those were hideous to behold and horribly bleared;

that a worthy dame she was may well, fore God,
>> be said!
> short body and thick waist,
> with bulging buttocks spread;
> more delicious to the taste
> was the one she by her led.

40 When Gawain glimpsed that gay lady that so gracious
>>>> looked,
with leave sought of the lord towards the ladies he went;
the elder he saluted, low to her bowing,
about the lovelier he laid then lightly his arms
and kissed her in courtly wise with courtesy speaking.
His acquaintance they requested, and quickly he begged
to be their servant in sooth, if so they desired.
They took him between them, and talking they led him
to a fireside in a fair room, and first of all called
for spices, which men sped without sparing to bring them,
and ever wine therewith well to their liking.
The lord for their delight leaped up full often,
many times merry games being minded to make;
his hood he doffed, and on high he hung it on a spear,
and offered it as an honour for any to win
who the most fun could devise at that Christmas feast –
'And I shall try, by my troth, to contend with the best
ere I forfeit this hood, with the help of my friends!'
Thus with laughter and jollity the lord made his jests
to gladden Sir Gawain with games that night
>> in hall,
> until the time was due
> that the lord for lights should call;
> Sir Gawain with leave withdrew
> and went to bed withal.

41 On the morn when every man remembers the time
    that our dear Lord for our doom to die was born,
    in every home wakes happiness on earth for His sake.
    So did it there on that day with the dearest delights:
    at each meal and at dinner marvellous dishes
    men set on the dais, the daintiest meats.
    The old ancient woman was highest at table,
    meetly to her side the master he took him;
    Gawain and the gay lady together were seated
    in the centre, where as was seemly the service began,
    and so on through the hall as honour directed.
    When each good man in his degree without grudge had
                             been served,
    there was food, there was festival, there was fullness of joy;
    and to tell all the tale of it I should tedious find,
    though pains I might take every point to detail.
    Yet I ween that Wawain and that woman so fair
    in companionship took such pleasure together
    in sweet society soft words speaking,
    their courteous converse clean and clear of all evil,
    that with their pleasant pastime no prince's sport
          compares.
      Drums beat, and trumps men wind,
      many pipers play their airs;
      each man his needs did mind,
      and they two minded theirs.

42 With much feasting they fared the first and the next day,
    and as heartily the third came hastening after:
    the gaiety of Saint John's day was glorious to hear;
    [with cheer of the choicest Childermas followed,]
    and that finished their revels, as folk there intended,
    for there were guests who must go in the grey morning.

So a wondrous wake they held, and the wine they drank,
and they danced and danced on, and dearly they carolled.
At last when it was late their leave then they sought
to wend on their ways, each worthy stranger.
Good-day then said Gawain, but the good man stayed him,
and led him to his own chamber to the chimney-corner,
and there he delayed him, and lovingly thanked him,
for the pride and pleasure his presence had brought,
for so honouring his house at that high season
and deigning his dwelling to adorn with his favour.
'Believe me, sir, while I live my luck I shall bless
that Gawain was my guest at God's own feast.'
'Gramercy, sir,' said Gawain, 'but the goodness is yours,
all the honour is your own – may the High King repay you!
And I am under your orders what you ask to perform,
as I am bound now to be, for better or worse,
> by right.'
> Him longer to retain
> the lord then pressed the knight;
> to him replied Gawain
> that he by no means might.

43 Then with courteous question he enquired of Gawain
what dire need had driven him on that festal date
with such keenness from the king's court, to come forth
> alone
ere wholly the holidays from men's homes had departed.
'In sooth, sir,' he said, 'you say but the truth:
a high errand and a hasty from that house brought me;
for I am summoned myself to seek for a place,
though I wonder where in the world I must wander to
> find it.
I would not miss coming nigh it on New Year's morning

for all the land in Logres, so our Lord help me!
And so, sir, this question I enquire of you here:
can you tell me in truth if you tale ever heard
of the Green Chapel, on what ground it may stand,
and of the great knight that guards it, all green in his colour?
For the terms of a tryst were between us established
to meet that man at that mark, if I remained alive,
and the named New Year is now nearly upon me,
and I would look on that lord, if God will allow me,
more gladly, by God's son, than gain any treasure.
So indeed, if you please, depart now I must.
For my business I have now but barely three days,
and I would fainer fall dead than fail in my errand.'
Then laughing said the lord: 'Now linger you must;
for when 'tis time to that tryst I will teach you the road.
On what ground is the Green Chapel – let it grieve you no
                                                        more!

In your bed you shall be, sir, till broad is the day,
without fret, and then fare on the first of the year,
and come to the mark at midmorn, there to make what
        play you know.
    Remain till New Year's day,
    then rise and riding go!
    We'll set you on your way,
    'tis but two miles or so.'

44 Then was Gawain delighted, and in gladness he laughed:
    'Now I thank you a thousand times for this beyond all!
    Now my quest is accomplished, as you crave it, I will
    dwell a few days here, and else do what you order.'
    The lord then seized him and set him in a seat beside him,
    and let the ladies be sent for to delight them the more,
    for their sweet pleasure there in peace by themselves.

For love of him that lord was as loud in his mirth
as one near out of his mind who scarce knew what he
                                                    meant.
Then he called to the knight, crying out loudly:
'You have promised to do whatever deed I propose.
Will you hold this behest here, at this moment?'
'Yes, certainly, sir,' then said the true knight,
'while I remain in your mansion, your command I'll obey.'
'Well,' returned he, 'you have travelled and toiled from afar,
and then I've kept you awake: you're not well yet, not cured;
both sustenance and sleep 'tis certain you need.
Upstairs you shall stay, sir, and stop there in comfort
tomorrow till Mass-time, and to a meal then go
when you wish with my wife, who with you shall sit
and comfort you with her company, till to court I return.
        You stay,
    and I shall early rouse,
    and a-hunting wend my way.'
    Gawain gracefully bows:
    'Your wishes I will obey.'

45 'One thing more,' said the master, 'we'll make an agreement:
whatever I win in the wood at once shall be yours,
and whatever gain you may get you shall give in exchange.
Shall we swap thus, sweet man – come, say what you think! –
whether one's luck be light, or one's lot be better?'
'By God,' quoth good Gawain, 'I agree to it all,
and whatever play you propose seems pleasant to me.'
'Done! 'Tis a bargain! Who'll bring us the drink?'
So said the lord of that land. They laughed one and all;
they drank and they dallied, and they did as they pleased,
these lords and ladies, as long as they wished,
and then with customs of France and many courtly phrases

they stood in sweet debate and soft words bandied,
and lovingly they kissed, their leave taking.
With trusty attendants and torches gleaming
they were brought at the last to their beds so soft,
   one and all.
 Yet ere to bed they came,
 he the bargain did oft recall;
 he knew how to play a game
 the old governor of that hall.

III

BEFORE the first daylight the folk uprose: the guests
that were to go for their grooms they called; and they
hurried up in haste horses to saddle, to stow all their
stuff and strap up their bags. The men of rank arrayed
them, for riding got ready, to saddle leaped swiftly, seized
then their bridles, and went off on their ways where their
wish was to go. The liege-lord of the land was not last of
them all to be ready to ride with a rout of his men; he ate a
hurried mouthful after the hearing of Mass, and with horn
to the hunting-field he hastened at once. When daylight
was opened yet dimly on earth he and his huntsmen were
up on their high horses. Then the leaders of the hounds
leashed them in couples, unclosed the kennel-door and
cried to them 'out!', and blew boldly on bugles three blasts
full long. Beagles bayed thereat, a brave noise making; and
they whipped and wheeled in those that wandered on a
scent; a hundred hunting-dogs, I have heard, of the best
   were they.
 To their stations keepers passed;
 the leashes were cast away,

and many a rousing blast
woke din in the woods that day.

47 At the first burst of the baying all beasts trembled;
deer dashed through the dale by dread bewildered,
and hastened to the heights, but they hotly were greeted,
and turned back by the beaters, who boldly shouted.
They let the harts go past with their high antlers,
and the brave bucks also with their branching palms;
for the lord of the castle had decreed in the close season
that no man should molest the male of the deer.
The hinds were held back with hey! and ware!,
the does driven with great din to the deep valleys:
there could be seen let slip a sleet of arrows;
at each turn under the trees went a twanging shaft
that into brown hides bit hard with barbéd head.
Lo! they brayed, and they bled, and on the banks they died;
and ever the hounds in haste hotly pursued them,
and hunters with high horns hurried behind them
with such a clamour and cry as if cliffs had been riven.
If any beast broke away from bowmen there shooting,
it was snatched down and slain at the receiving-station;
when they had been harried from the height and hustled to
the waters
the men were so wise in their craft at the watches below,
and their greyhounds were so great that they got them at
once,
and flung them down in a flash, as fast as men could see
with sight.
The lord then wild for joy
did oft spur and oft alight,
and thus in bliss employ
that day till dark of night.

48 Thus in his game the lord goes under greenwood eaves,
and Gawain the bold lies in goodly bed,
lazing, till the walls are lit by the light of day,
under costly coverlet with curtains about him.
And as in slumber he strayed, he heard stealthily come
a soft sound at his door as it secretly opened;
and from under the clothes he craned then his head,
a corner of the curtain he caught up a little,
and looked that way warily to learn what it was.
It was the lady herself, most lovely to see,
that cautiously closed the door quietly behind her,
and drew near to his bed. Then abashed was the knight,
and lay down swiftly to look as if he slept;
and she stepped silently and stole to his bed,
cast back the curtain, and crept then within,
and sat her down softly on the side of the bed,
and there lingered very long to look for his waking.
He lay there lurking a long while and wondered,
and mused in his mind how the matter would go,
to what point it might pass – to some surprise, he fancied.
Yet he said to himself: 'More seemly 'twould be
in due course with question to enquire what she wishes.'
Then rousing he rolled over, and round to her turning
he lifted his eyelids with a look as of wonder,
and signed him with the cross, thus safer to be kept
    aright.
  With chin and cheeks so sweet
  of blended red and white,
  with grace then him did greet
  small lips with laughter bright.

49 'Good morning, Sir Gawain!' said that gracious lady.
'You are a careless sleeper, if one can creep on you so!

Now quickly you are caught! If we come not to terms,
I shall bind you in your bed, you may be assured.'
With laughter the lady thus lightly jested.
'Good morning to your grace!' said Gawain gaily.
'You shall work on me your will, and well I am pleased;
for I submit immediately, and for mercy I cry,
and that is best, as I deem, for I am obliged to do so.'
Thus he jested in return with much gentle laughter:
'But if you would, lady gracious, then leave grant me,
and release your prisoner and pray him to rise,
I would abandon this bed and better array me;
the more pleasant would it prove then to parley with you.'
'Nay, for sooth, fair sir,' said the sweet lady,
'you shall not go from your bed! I will govern you better:
here fast shall I enfold you, on the far side also,
and then talk with my true knight that I have taken so.
For I wot well indeed that Sir Wawain you are,
to whom all men pay homage wherever you ride;
your honour, your courtesy, by the courteous is praised,
by lords, by ladies, by all living people.
And right here you now are, and we all by ourselves;
my husband and his huntsmen far hence have ridden,
other men are abed, and my maids also,
the door closed and caught with a clasp that is strong;
and since I have in this house one that all delight in,
my time to account I will turn, while for talk I chance
         have still.
   To my body will you welcome be
   of delight to take your fill;
   for need constraineth me
   to serve you, and I will.'

50 'Upon my word,' said Gawain, 'that is well, I guess;
     though I am not now he of whom you are speaking –
     to attain to such honour as here you tell of
     I am a knight unworthy, as well indeed I know –
     by God, I would be glad, if good to you seemed
     whatever I could say, or in service could offer
     to the pleasure of your excellence – it would be pure delight.'
     'In good faith, Sir Gawain,' said the gracious lady,
     'the prowess and the excellence that all others approve,
     if I scorned or decried them, it were scant courtesy.
     But there are ladies in number who liever would now
     have thee in their hold, sir, as I have thee here,
     pleasantly to play with in polished converse,
     their solace to seek and their sorrows to soothe,
     than great part of the goods or gold that they own.
     But I thank Him who on high of Heaven is Lord
     that I have here wholly in my hand what all desire,
            by grace.'
        She was an urgent wooer,
        that lady fair of face;
        the knight with speeches pure
        replied in every case.

51 'Madam,' said he merrily, 'Mary reward you!
     For I have enjoyed, in good faith, your generous favour,
     and much honour have had else from others' kind deeds;
     but as for the courtesy they accord me, since my claim is
                                                    not equal,
     the honour is your own, who are ever well-meaning.'
     'Nay, Mary!' the lady demurred, 'as for me, I deny it.
     For were I worth all the legion of women alive,
     and all the wealth in the world at my will possessed,
     if I should exchange at my choice and choose me a husband,

for the noble nature I know, Sir Knight, in thee here,
in beauty and bounty and bearing so gay –
of which earlier I have heard, and hold it now true –
then no lord alive would I elect before you.'
'In truth, lady,' he returned, 'you took one far better.
But I am proud of the praise you are pleased to give me,
and as your servant in earnest my sovereign I hold you,
and your knight I become, and may Christ reward you.'
Thus of many matters they spoke till midmorn was passed,
and ever the lady demeaned her as one that loved him much,
and he fenced with her featly, ever flawless in manner.
'Though I were lady most lovely,' thought the lady to
                                                    herself,
'the less love would he bring here,' since he looked for
        his bane, that blow
    that him so soon should grieve,
    and needs it must be so.
    Then the lady asked for leave
    and at once he let her go.

52 Then she gave him 'good day', and with a glance she
                                                    laughed,
    and as she stood she astonished him with the strength of
                                                    her words:
    'Now He that prospers all speech for this disport repay you!
    But that you should be Gawain, it gives me much thought.'
    'Why so?', then eagerly the knight asked her,
    afraid that he had failed in the form of his converse.
    But 'God bless you! For this reason', blithely she answered,
    'that one so good as Gawain the gracious is held,
    who all the compass of courtesy includes in his person,
    so long with a lady could hardly have lingered
    without craving a kiss, as a courteous knight,

67

by some tactful turn that their talk led to.'
Then said Wawain, 'Very well, as you wish be it done.
I will kiss at your command, as becometh a knight,
and more, lest he displease you, so plead it no longer.'
She came near thereupon and caught him in her arms,
and down daintily bending dearly she kissed him.
They courteously commended each other to Christ.
Without more ado through the door she withdrew and
                                                    departed,
and he to rise up in haste made ready at once.
He calls to his chamberlain, and chooses his clothes,
and goes forth when garbed all gladly to Mass.
Then he went to a meal that meetly awaited him,
and made merry all day, till the moon arose
        o'er earth.
   Ne'er was knight so gaily engaged
   between two dames of worth,
   the youthful and the aged:
   together they made much mirth.

53 And ever the lord of the land in his delight was abroad,
    hunting by holt and heath after hinds that were barren.
    When the sun began to slope he had slain such a number
    of does and other deer one might doubt it were true.
    Then the fell folk at last came flocking all in,
    and quickly of the kill they a quarry assembled.
    Thither the master hastened with a host of his men,
    gathered together those greatest in fat
    and had them riven open rightly, as the rules require.
    At the assay they were searched by some that were there,
    and two fingers' breadth of fat they found in the leanest.
    Next they slit the eslot, seized on the arber,
    shaved it with a sharp knife and shore away the grease;

next ripped the four limbs and rent off the hide.
Then they broke open the belly, the bowels they removed
(flinging them nimbly afar) and the flesh of the knot;
they grasped then the gorge, disengaging with skill
the weasand from the windpipe, and did away with the guts.
Then they shore out the shoulders with their sharpened
knives
(drawing the sinews through a small cut) the sides to keep
whole;
next they burst open the breast, and broke it apart,
and again at the gorge one begins thereupon,
cuts all up quickly till he comes to the fork,
and fetches forth the fore-numbles; and following after
all the tissues along the ribs they tear away quickly.
Thus by the bones of the back they broke off with skill,
down even to the haunch, all that hung there together,
and hoisted it up all whole and hewed it off there:
and that they took for the numbles, as I trow is their
> name in kind.
>> Along the fork of every thigh
>> the flaps they fold behind;
>> to hew it in two they hie,
>> down the back all to unbind.

54 Both the head and the neck they hew off after,
and next swiftly they sunder the sides from the chine,
and the bone for the crow they cast in the boughs.
Then they thrust through both thick sides with a thong by
the rib,
and then by the hocks of the legs they hang them both up:
all the folk earn the fees that fall to their lot.
Upon the fell of the fair beast they fed their hounds then
on the liver and the lights and the leather of the paunches

with bread bathed in blood blended amongst them.
Boldly they blew the prise, amid the barking of dogs,
and then bearing up their venison bent their way homeward,
striking up strongly many a stout horn-call.
When daylight was done they all duly were come
into the noble castle, where quietly the knight
      abode
  in bliss by bright fire set.
  Thither the lord now strode;
  when Gawain with him met,
  then free all pleasure flowed.

55 Then the master commanded his men to meet in that hall,
and both dames to come down with their damsels also;
before all the folk on that floor fair men he ordered
to fetch there forthwith his venison before him,
and all gracious in game to Gawain he called,
announced the number by tally of the nimble beasts,
and showed him the shining fat all shorn on the ribs.
'How does this play please you? Have I praise deserved?
Have I earned by mine art the heartiest thanks?'
'Yea verily,' the other averred, 'here is venison the fairest
that I've seen in seven years in the season of winter!'
'And I give it you all, Gawain,' said the good man at once,
'for as our covenant accorded you may claim it as your own.'
'That is true,' he returned, 'and I tell you the same:
what of worth within these walls I have won also
with as good will, I warrant, 'tis awarded to you.'
His fair neck he enfolded then fast in his arms,
and kissed him with all the kindness that his courtesy knew.
'There take you my gains, sir! I got nothing more.
I would give it up gladly even if greater it were.'

'That is a good one!' quoth the good man. 'Greatly I thank
　　　　　　　　　　you.
'Tis such, maybe, that you had better briefly now tell me
where you won this same wealth by the wits you possess.'
'That was not the covenant,' quoth he. 'Do not question
　　　　　　　　　　me more!
For you've drawn what is due to you, no doubt can you
　　　　have 'tis true.'
　　　They laugh, and with voices fair
　　　their merriment pursue,
　　　and to supper soon repair
　　　with many dainties new.

56　Later by the chimney in chamber they were seated,
　　abundant wine of the best was brought to them oft,
　　and again as a game they agreed on the morrow
　　to abide by the same bond as they had bargained before:
　　chance what might chance, to exchange all their trade,
　　whatever new thing they got, when they gathered at night.
　　They concluded this compact before the courtiers all;
　　the drink for the bargain was brought forth in jest;
　　then their leave at the last they lovingly took,
　　and away then at once each went to his bed.
　　When the cock had crowed and cackled but thrice,
　　the lord had leaped from his bed, and his lieges each one;
　　so that their meal had been made, and the Mass was over,
　　and folk bound for the forest, ere the first daybreak,
　　　　　to chase.
　　　Loud with hunters and horns
　　　o'er plains they passed apace,
　　　and loosed there among the thorns
　　　the running dogs to race.

57 Soon these cried for a quest in a covert by a marsh;
   the huntsman hailed the hound that first heeded the scent,
   stirring words he spoke to him with a strident voice.
   The hounds then that heard it hastened thither swiftly,
   and fell fast on the line, some forty at once.
   Then such a baying and babel of bloodhounds together
   arose that the rock-wall rang all about them.
   Hunters enheartened them with horn and with mouth,
   and then all in a rout rushed on together
   between a fen-pool in that forest and a frowning crag.
   In a tangle under a tall cliff at the tarn's edges,
   where the rough rock ruggedly in ruin was fallen,
   they fared to the find, followed by hunters
   who made a cast round the crag and the clutter of stones,
   till well they were aware that it waited within:
   the very beast that the baying bloodhounds had spoken.
   Then they beat on the bushes and bade him uprise,
   and forth he came to their peril against folk in his path.
   'Twas a boar without rival that burst out upon them;
   long the herd he had left, that lone beast aged,
   for savage was he, of all swine the hugest,
   grim indeed when he grunted. Then aghast were many;
   for three at the first thrust he threw to the ground,
   and sprang off with great speed, sparing the others;
   and they hallooed on high, and ha! ha! shouted,
   and held horn to mouth, blowing hard the rally.
   Many were the wild mouthings of men and of dogs,
   as they bounded after this boar, him with blare and with
           din to quell.
       Many times he turns to bay,
       and maims the pack pell-mell;
       he hurts many hounds, and they
       grievously yowl and yell.

58 Hunters then hurried up eager to shoot him,
    aimed at him their arrows, often they hit him;
    but poor at core proved the points that pitched on his
                                 shields,
    and the barbs on his brows would bite not at all;
    though the shaven shaft shivered in pieces,
    back the head came hopping, wherever it hit him.
    But when the hurts went home of their heavier strokes,
    then with brain wild for battle he burst out upon them,
    ruthless he rent them as he rushed forward,
    and many quailed at his coming and quickly withdrew.
    But the lord on a light horse went leaping after him;
    as bold man on battle-field with his bugle he blew
    the rally-call as he rode through the rough thickets,
    pursuing this wild swine till the sunbeams slanted.
    This day in such doings thus duly they passed,
    while our brave knight beloved there lies in his bed
    at home in good hap, in housings so costly and gay.
        The lady did not forget:
        she came to bid good day;
        early she on him set,
        his will to wear away.

59 She passed to the curtain and peeped at the knight.
    Sir Wawain graciously then welcomed her first,
    and she answered him alike, eagerly speaking,
    and sat her softly by his side; and suddenly she laughed,
    and with a look full of love delivered these words:
    'Sir, if you are Wawain, a wonder I think it
    that a man so well-meaning, ever mindful of good,
    yet cannot comprehend the customs of the gentle;
    and if one acquaints you therewith, you do not keep them
                              in mind:

thou hast forgot altogether what a day ago I taught
by the plainest points I could put into words!'
'What is that?' he said at once. 'I am not aware of it at all.
But if you are telling the truth, I must take all the blame.'
'And yet as to kisses', she quoth, 'this counsel I gave you:
wherever favour is found, defer not to claim them:
that becomes all who care for courteous manners.'
'Take back', said the true knight, 'that teaching, my dear!
For that I dared not do, for dread of refusal.
Were I rebuffed, I should be to blame for so bold an offer.'
'Ma fay!' said the fair lady, 'you may not be refused;
you are stout enough to constrain one by strength, if you
                                               like,
if any were so ill bred as to answer you nay.'
'Indeed, by God', quoth Gawain, 'you graciously speak;
but force finds no favour among the folk where I dwell,
and any gift not given gladly and freely.
I am at your call and command to kiss when you please.
You may receive as you desire, and cease as you think
    in place.'
      Then down the lady bent,
      and sweetly kissed his face.
      Much speech then there they spent
      of lovers' grief and grace.

60 'I would learn from you, lord,' the lady then said,
'if you would not mind my asking, what is the meaning of
                                               this:
that one so young as are you in years, and so gay,
by renown so well known for knighthood and breeding,
while of all chivalry the choice, the chief thing to praise,
is the loyal practice of love: very lore of knighthood –
for, talking of the toils that these true knights suffer,

it is the title and contents and text of their works:
how lovers for their true love their lives have imperilled,
have endured for their dear one dolorous trials,
until avenged by their valour, their adversity passed,
they have brought bliss into her bower by their own brave
virtues –

and you are the knight of most noble renown in our age,
and your fame and fair name afar is published,
and I have sat by your very self now for the second time,
yet your mouth has never made any remark I have heard
that ever belonged to love-making, lesser or greater.
Surely, you that are so accomplished and so courtly in
your vows

should be prompt to expound to a young pupil
by signs and examples the science of lovers.
Why? Are you ignorant who all honour enjoy?
Or else you esteem me too stupid to understand your
      courtship?
    But nay!
    Here single I come and sit,
    a pupil for your play;
    come, teach me of your wit,
    while my lord is far away.'

61   'In good faith', said Gawain, 'may God reward you!
    Great delight I gain, and am glad beyond measure
    that one so worthy as you should be willing to come here
    and take pains with so poor a man: as for playing with
your knight,

    showing favour in any form, it fills me with joy.
    But for me to take up the task on true love to lecture,
    to comment on the text and tales of knighthood
    to you, who I am certain possess far more skill

in that art by the half than a hundred of such
as I am, or shall ever be while on earth I remain,
it would be folly manifold, in faith, my lady!
All your will I would wish to work, as I am able,
being so beholden in honour, and, so help me the Lord,
desiring ever the servant of yourself to remain.'
Thus she tested and tried him, tempting him often,
so as to allure him to love-making, whatever lay in her heart.
But his defence was so fair that no fault could be seen,
nor any evil upon either side, nor aught but joy
   they wist.
  They laughed and long they played;
  at last she him then kissed,
  with grace adieu him bade,
  and went whereso she list.

62 Then rousing from his rest he rose to hear Mass,
and then their dinner was laid and daintily served.
The livelong day with the ladies in delight he spent,
but the lord o'er the lands leaped to and fro,
pursuing his fell swine that o'er the slopes hurtled
and bit asunder the backs of the best of his hounds,
wherever to bay he was brought, until bowmen dislodged
              him,
and made him, maugre his teeth, move again onward,
so fast the shafts flew when the folk were assembled.
And yet the stoutest of them still he made start there aside,
till at last he was so spent he could speed no further,
but in such haste as he might he made for a hollow
on a reef beside a rock where the river was flowing.
He put the bank at his back, began then to paw;
fearfully the froth of his mouth foamed from the corners;
he whetted his white tusks. Then weary were all

the brave men so bold as by him to stand
of plaguing him from afar, yet for peril they dared not
      come nigher.
    He had hurt so many before,
    that none had now desire
    to be torn with the tusks once more
    of a beast both mad and dire.

63 Till the knight himself came, his courser spurring,
   and saw him brought there to bay, and all about him his
                                   men.

Nothing loth he alighted, and leaving his horse,
brandished a bright blade and boldly advanced,
striding stoutly through the ford to where stood the felon.
The wild beast was aware of him with his weapon in hand,
and high raised his hair; with such hate he snorted
that folk feared for the knight, lest his foe should worst him.
Out came the swine and set on him at once,
and the boar and the brave man were both in a mellay
in the wildest of the water. The worse had the beast,
for the man marked him well, and as they met he at once
struck steadily his point straight in the neck-slot,
and hit him up to the hilts, so that his heart was riven,
and with a snarl he succumbed, and was swept down the
      water straightway.
    A hundred hounds him caught,
    and fiercely bit their prey;
    the men to the bank him brought,
    and dogs him dead did lay.

64 There men blew for the prise in many a blaring horn,
   and high and loud hallooed all the hunters that could;
   bloodhounds bayed for the beast, as bade the masters,

who of that hard-run chase were the chief huntsmen.
Then one that was well learnéd in woodmen's lore
with pretty cunning began to carve up this boar.
First he hewed off his head and on high set it,
then he rent him roughly down the ridge of the back,
brought out the bowels, burned them on gledes,
and with them, blended with blood, the bloodhounds
                                                    rewarded.

Next he broke up the boar-flesh in broad slabs of brawn,
and haled forth the hastlets in order all duly,
and yet all whole he fastened the halves together,
and strongly on a stout pole he strung them then up.
Now with this swine homeward swiftly they hastened,
and the boar's head was borne before the brave knight
                                                    himself
who felled him in the ford by force of his hand
        so great.
    Until he saw Sir Gawain
    in the hall he could hardly wait.
    He called, and his pay to gain
    the other came there straight.

65 The lord with his loud voice and laughter merry
    gaily he greeted him when Gawain he saw.
    The fair ladies were fetched and the folk all assembled,
    and he showed them the shorn slabs, and shaped his report
    of the width and wondrous length, and the wickedness also
    in war, of the wild swine, as in the woods he had fled.
    With fair words his friend the feat then applauded,
    and praised the great prowess he had proved in his deeds;
    for such brawn on a beast, the brave knight declared,
    or such sides on a swine he had never seen before.
    They then handled the huge head, and highly he praised it,

showing horror at the hideous thing to honour the lord.
'Now, Gawain,' said the good man, 'this game is your own
by close covenant we concluded, as clearly you know.'
'That is true,' he returned, 'and as truly I assure you
all my winnings, I warrant, I shall award you in exchange.'
He clasped his neck, and courteously a kiss he then gave
him

and swiftly with a second he served him on the spot.
'Now we are quits,' he quoth, 'and clear for this evening
of all covenants we accorded, since I came to this house,
      as is due.'
   The lord said: 'By Saint Gile,
   your match I never knew!
   You'll be wealthy in a while,
   such trade if you pursue.'

66 Then on top of the trestles the tables they laid,
cast the cloths thereon, and clear light then
wakened along the walls; waxen torches
men set there, and servants went swift about the hall.
Much gladness and gaiety began then to spring
round the fire on the hearth, and freely and oft
at supper and later: many songs of delight,
such as canticles of Christmas, and new carol-dances,
amid all the mannerly mirth that men can tell of;
and ever our noble knight was next to the lady.
Such glances she gave him of her gracious favour,
secretly stealing sweet looks that strong man to charm,
that he was passing perplexed, and ill-pleased at heart.
Yet he would fain not of his courtesy coldly refuse her,
but graciously engaged her, however against the grain
      the play.
   When mirth they had made in hall

as long as they wished to stay,
to a room did the lord them call
and to the ingle they made their way.

67 There amid merry words and wine they had a mind once
                                                    more
to harp on the same note on New Year's Eve.
But said Gawain: 'Grant me leave to go on the morrow!
For the appointment approaches that I pledged myself to.'
The lord was loth to allow it, and longer would keep him,
and said: 'As I am a true man I swear on my troth
the Green Chapel thou shalt gain, and go to your business
in the dawn of New Year, sir, ere daytime begins.
So still lie upstairs and stay at thine ease,
and I shall hunt in the holt here, and hold to my terms
with thee truly, when I return, to trade all our gains.
For I have tested thee twice, and trusty I find thee.
Now "third time pays for all", bethink thee tomorrow!
Make we merry while we may and be mindful of joy,
for the woe one may win whenever one wishes!'
This was graciously agreed, and Gawain would linger.
Then gaily drink is given them and they go to their beds
          with light.
    Sir Gawain lies and sleeps
    soft and sound all night;
    his host to his hunting keeps,
    and is early arrayed aright.

68 After Mass of a morsel he and his men partook.
Merry was the morning. For his mount then he called.
All the huntsmen that on horse behind him should follow
were ready mounted to ride arrayed at the gates.
Wondrous fair were the fields, for the frost clung there;

in red rose-hued o'er the wrack arises the sun,
sailing clear along the coasts of the cloudy heavens.
The hunters loosed hounds by a holt-border;
the rocks rang in the wood to the roar of their horns.
Some fell on the line to where the fox was lying,
crossing and re-crossing it in the cunning of their craft.
A hound then gives tongue, the huntsman names him,
round him press his companions in a pack all snuffling,
running forth in a rabble then right in his path.
The fox flits before them. They find him at once,
and when they see him by sight they pursue him hotly,
decrying him full clearly with a clamour of wrath.
He dodges and ever doubles through many a dense coppice,
and looping oft he lurks and listens under fences.
At last at a little ditch he leaps o'er a thorn-hedge,
sneaks out secretly by the side of a thicket,
weens he is out of the wood and away by his wiles from the
                                        hounds.
Thus he went unawares to a watch that was posted,
where fierce on him fell three foes at once
          all grey.
     He swerves then swift again,
     and dauntless darts astray;
     in grief and in great pain
     to the wood he turns away.

69 Then to hark to the hounds it was heart's delight,
when all the pack came upon him, there pressing together.
Such a curse at the view they called down on him
that the clustering cliffs might have clattered in ruin.
Here he was hallooed when hunters came on him,
yonder was he assailed with snarling tongues;
there he was threatened and oft thief was he called,

81

with ever the trailers at his tail so that tarry he could not.
Oft was he run at, if he rushed outwards;
oft he swerved in again, so subtle was Reynard.
Yea! he led the lord and his hunt as laggards behind him
thus by mount and by hill till mid-afternoon.
Meanwhile the courteous knight in the castle in comfort
                slumbered
behind the comely curtains in the cold morning.
But the lady in love-making had no liking to sleep
nor to disappoint the purpose she had planned in her heart;
but rising up swiftly his room now she sought
in a gay mantle that to the ground was measured
and was fur-lined most fairly with fells well trimmed,
with no comely coif on her head, only the clear jewels
that were twined in her tressure by twenties in clusters;
her noble face and her neck all naked were laid,
her breast bare in front and at the back also.
She came through the chamber-door and closed it behind
                her,
wide set a window, and to wake him she called,
thus greeting him gaily with her gracious words
    of cheer:
    'Ah! man, how canst thou sleep,
    the morning is so clear!'
    He lay in darkness deep,
    but her call he then could hear.

70 In heavy darkness drowsing he dream-words muttered,
as a man whose mind was bemused with many mournful
                thoughts,
how destiny should his doom on that day bring him
when he at the Green Chapel the great man would meet,
and be obliged his blow to abide without debate at all.

But when so comely she came, he recalled then his wits,
swept aside his slumbers, and swiftly made answer.
The lady in lovely guise came laughing sweetly,
bent down o'er his dear face, and deftly kissed him.
He greeted her graciously with a glad welcome,
seeing her so glorious and gaily attired,
so faultless in her features and so fine in her hues
that at once joy up-welling went warm to his heart.
With smiles sweet and soft they turned swiftly to mirth,
and only brightness and bliss was broached there between
      them so gay.
   They spoke then speeches good,
   much pleasure was in that play;
   great peril between them stood,
   unless Mary for her knight should pray.

71 For she, queenly and peerless, pressed him so closely,
led him so near the line, that at last he must needs
either refuse her with offence or her favours there take.
He cared for his courtesy, lest a caitiff he proved,
yet more for his sad case, if he should sin commit
and to the owner of the house, to his host, be a traitor.
'God help me!' said he. 'Happen that shall not!'
Smiling sweetly aside from himself then he turned
all the fond words of favour that fell from her lips.
Said she to the knight then: 'Now shame you deserve,
if you love not one that lies alone here beside you,
who beyond all women in the world is wounded in heart,
unless you have a lemman, more beloved, whom you like
                        better,
and have affianced faith to that fair one so fast and so true
that your release you desire not – and so I believe now;
and to tell me if that be so truly, I beg you.

For all sakes that men swear by conceal not the truth
      in guile.'
  The knight said: 'By Saint John,'
  and softly gave a smile,
  'Nay! lover have I none,
  and none will have meanwhile.'

72 'Those words', said the woman, 'are the worst that could be.
But I am answered indeed, and 'tis hard to endure.
Kiss me now kindly, and I will quickly depart.
I may but mourn while I live as one that much is in love.'
Sighing she sank down, and sweetly she kissed him;
then soon she left his side, and said as she stood there:
'Now, my dear, at this parting do me this pleasure,
give me something as thy gift, thy glove it might be,
that I may remember thee, dear man, my mourning to
                        lessen.'
'Now on my word,' then said he, 'I wish I had here
the loveliest thing for thy delight that in my land I possess;
for worthily have you earned wondrously often
more reward by rights than within my reach would now be,
save to allot you as love-token thing of little value.
Beneath your honour it is to have here and now
a glove for a guerdon as the gift of Sir Gawain:
and I am here on an errand in unknown lands,
and have no bearers with baggage and beautiful things
(unluckily, dear lady) for your delight at this time.
A man must do as he is placed; be not pained nor
      aggrieved,' said he.
  Said she so comely clad:
  'Nay, noble knight and free,
  though naught of yours I had,
  you should get a gift from me.'

73 A rich ring she offered him of red gold fashioned,
    with a stone like a star standing up clear
    that bore brilliant beams as bright as the sun:
    I warrant you it was worth wealth beyond measure.
    But the knight said nay to it, and announced then at once:
    'I will have no gifts, fore God, of your grace at this time.
    I have none to return you, and naught will I take.'
    She proffered it and pressed him, and he her pleading
                         refused,
    and swore swiftly upon his word that accept it he would not.
    And she, sorry that he refused, said to him further:
    'If to my ring you say nay, since too rich it appears,
    and you would not so deeply be indebted to me,
    I shall give you my girdle, less gain will that be.'
    She unbound a belt swiftly that embracing her sides
    was clasped above her kirtle under her comely mantle.
    Fashioned it was of green silk, and with gold finished,
    though only braided round about, embroidered by hand;
    and this she would give to Gawain, and gladly besought him,
    of no worth though it were, to be willing to take it.
    And he said nay, he would not, he would never receive
    either gold or jewelry, ere God the grace sent him
    to accomplish the quest on which he had come thither.
    'And therefore I pray you, please be not angry,
    and cease to insist on it, for to your suit I will ever
        say no.
      I am deeply in debt to you
      for the favour that you show,
      to be your servant true
      for ever in weal or woe.'

74 'Do you refuse now this silk,' said the fair lady,
    'because in itself it is poor? And so it appears.

See how small 'tis in size, and smaller in value!
But one who knew of the nature that is knit therewithin
would appraise it probably at a price far higher.
For whoever goes girdled with this green riband,
while he keeps it well clasped closely about him,
there is none so hardy under heaven that to hew him were
                                        able;
for he could not be killed by any cunning of hand.'
The knight then took note, and thought now in his heart,
'twould be a prize in that peril that was appointed to him.
When he gained the Green Chapel to get there his sentence,
if by some sleight he were not slain, 'twould be a sovereign
                                        device.
Then he bore with her rebuke, and debated not her words;
and she pressed on him the belt, and proffered it in earnest;
and he agreed, and she gave it very gladly indeed,
and prayed him for her sake to part with it never,
but on his honour hide it from her husband; and he then
                                        agreed
that no one ever should know, nay, none in the world
        but they.
    With earnest heart and mood
    great thanks he oft did say.
    She then the knight so good
    a third time kissed that day.

75 Then she left him alone, her leave taking,
    for amusement from the man no more could she get.
    When she was gone Sir Gawain got him soon ready,
    arose and robed himself in raiment noble.
    He laid up the love-lace that the lady had given,
    hiding it heedfully where he after might find it.
    Then first of all he chose to fare to the chapel,

privately approached a priest, and prayed that he there
would uplift his life, that he might learn better
how his soul should be saved, when he was sent from the
world.
There he cleanly confessed him and declared his misdeeds,
both the more and the less, and for mercy he begged,
to absolve him of them all he besought the good man;
and he assoiled him and made him as safe and as clean
as for Doom's Day indeed, were it due on the morrow.
Thereafter more merry he made among the fair ladies,
with carol-dances gentle and all kinds of rejoicing,
than ever he did ere that day, till the darkness of night,
     in bliss.
  Each man there said: 'I vow
  a delight to all he is!
  Since hither he came till now,
  he was ne'er so gay as this.'

76 Now indoors let him dwell and have dearest delight,
while the free lord yet fares afield in his sports!
At last the fox he has felled that he followed so long;
for, as he spurred through a spinney to espy there the villain,
where the hounds he had heard that hard on him pressed,
Reynard on his road came through a rough thicket,
and all the rabble in a rush were right on his heels.
The man is aware of the wild thing, and watchful awaits
him,
brings out his bright brand and at the beast hurls it;
and he blenched at the blade, and would have backed if he
could.
A hound hastened up, and had him ere he could;
and right before the horse's feet they fell on him all,
and worried there the wily one with a wild clamour.

87

The lord quickly alights and lifts him at once,
snatching him swiftly from their slavering mouths,
holds him high o'er his head, hallooing loudly;
and there bay at him fiercely many furious hounds.
Huntsmen hurried thither, with horns full many
ever sounding the assembly, till they saw the master.
When together had come his company noble,
all that ever bore bugle were blowing at once,
and all the others hallooed that had not a horn:
it was the merriest music that ever men harkened,
the resounding song there raised that for Reynard's soul
      awoke.
   To hounds they pay their fees,
   their heads they fondly stroke,
   and Reynard then they seize,
   and off they skin his cloak.

77 And then homeward they hastened, for at hand was now
                              night,
making strong music on their mighty horns.
The lord alighted at last at his beloved abode,
found a fire in the hall, and fair by the hearth
Sir Gawain the good, and gay was he too,
among the ladies in delight his lot was most joyful.
He was clad in a blue cloak that came to the ground;
his surcoat well beseemed him with its soft lining,
and its hood of like hue that hung on his shoulder:
all fringed with white fur very finely were both.
He met indeed the master in the midst of the floor,
and in gaiety greeted him, and graciously said:
'In this case I will first our covenant fulfil
that to our good we agreed, when ungrudged went the
                            drink.'

He clasps then the knight and kisses him thrice,
as long and deliciously as he could lay them upon him.
'By Christ!' the other quoth, 'you've come by a fortune
in winning such wares, were they worth what you paid.'
'Indeed, the price was not important,' promptly he
            answered,
'whereas plainly is paid now the profit I gained.'
'Marry!' said the other man, 'mine is not up to't;
for I have hunted all this day, and naught else have I got
but this foul fox-fell – the Fiend have the goods! –
and that is price very poor to pay for such treasures
as these you have thrust upon me, three such kisses
   so good.'
  ''Tis enough,' then said Gawain.
  'I thank you, by the Rood,'
  and how the fox was slain
  he told him as they stood.

78 With mirth and minstrelsy and meats at their pleasure
as merry they made as any men could be;
amid the laughter of ladies and light words of jest
both Gawain and the good man could no gayer have
            proved,
unless they had doted indeed or else drunken had been.
Both the host and his household went on with their games,
till the hour had approached when part must they all;
to bed were now bound the brave folk at last.
Bowing low his leave of the lord there first
the good knight then took, and graciously thanked him:
'For such a wondrous welcome as within these walls I have
            had,
for your honour at this high feast the High King reward you!
In your service I set myself, your servant, if you will.

For I must needs make a move tomorrow, as you know,
if you give me some good man to go, as you promised,
and guide me to the Green Chapel, as God may permit me
to face on New Year's day such doom as befalls me.'
'On my word,' said his host, 'with hearty good will
to all that ever I promised I promptly shall hold.'
Then a servant he assigns him to set him on the road,
and by the downs to conduct him, that without doubt or
delay
he might through wild and through wood ways most
      straight pursue.
   Said Gawain, 'My thanks receive,
   such a favour you will do!'
   The knight then took his leave
   of those noble ladies two.

79 Sadly he kissed them and said his farewells,
and pressed oft upon them in plenty his thanks,
and they promptly the same again repaid him;
to God's keeping they gave him, grievously sighing.
Then from the people of the castle he with courtesy parted;
all the men that he met he remembered with thanks
for their care for his comfort and their kind service,
and the trouble each had taken in attendance upon him;
and every one was as woeful to wish him adieu
as had they lived all their lives with his lordship in honour.
Then with link-men and lights he was led to his chamber
and brought sweetly to bed, there to be at his rest.
That soundly he slept then assert will I not,
for he had many matters in the morning to mind, if he
      would, in thought.
   There let him lie in peace,
   near now is the tryst he sought.

If a while you will hold your peace,
I will tell the deeds they wrought!

IV

Now New Year draws near and the night passes, day comes driving the dark, as ordained by God; but wild weathers of the world awake in the land, clouds cast keenly the cold upon earth with bitter breath from the North biting the naked. Snow comes shivering sharp to shrivel the wild things, the whistling wind whirls from the heights and drives every dale full of drifts very deep. Long the knight listens as he lies in his bed; though he lays down his eyelids, very little he sleeps: at the crow of every cock he recalls well his tryst. Briskly he rose from his bed ere the break of day, for there was light from a lamp that illumined his chamber. He called to his chamberlain, who quickly him answered, and he bade him bring his byrnie and his beast saddle. The man got him up and his gear fetched him, and garbed then Sir Gawain in great array; first he clad him in his clothes to keep out the cold, and after that in his harness that with heed had been tended, both his pauncer and his plates polished all brightly, the rings rid of the rust on his rich byrnie: all was neat as if new, and the

knight him

thanked with delight.
He put on every piece
all burnished well and bright;
most gallant from here to Greece
for his courser called the knight.

81 While the proudest of his apparel he put on himself:
  his coat-armour, with the cognisance of the clear symbol
  upon velvet environed with virtuous gems
  all bound and braided about it, with broidered seams
  and with fine furs lined wondrous fairly within,
  yet he overlooked not the lace that the lady had given him;
  that Gawain forgot not, of his own good thinking;
  when he had belted his brand upon his buxom haunches,
  he twined the love-token twice then about him,
  and swiftly he swathed it sweetly about his waist,
  that girdle of green silk, and gallant it looked
  upon the royal red cloth that was rich to behold.
  But he wore not for worth nor for wealth this girdle,
  not for pride in the pendants, though polished they were,
  not though the glittering gold there gleamed at the ends,
  but so that himself he might save when suffer he must,
  must abide bane without debating it with blade or with
          brand of war.
      When arrayed the knight so bold
      came out before the door,
      to all that high household
      great thanks he gave once more.

82 Now Gringolet was groomed, the great horse and high,
  who had been lodged to his liking and loyally tended:
  fain to gallop was that gallant horse for his good fettle.
  His master to him came and marked well his coat,
  and said: 'Now solemnly myself I swear on my troth
  there is a company in this castle that is careful of honour!
  Their lord that them leads, may his lot be joyful!
  Their beloved lady in life may delight befall her!
  If they out of charity thus cherish a guest,
  upholding their house in honour, may He them reward

that upholds heaven on high, and all of you too!
And if life a little longer I might lead upon earth,
I would give you some guerdon gladly, were I able.'
Then he steps in the stirrup and strides on his horse;
his shield his man showed him, and on shoulder he slung it,
Gringolet he goaded with his gilded heels,
and he plunged forth on the pavement, and prancing no
      more stood there.
    Ready now was his squire to ride
    that his helm and lance would bear.
    'Christ keep this castle!' he cried
    and wished it fortune fair.

83   The bridge was brought down and the broad gates then
    unbarred and swung back upon both hinges.
    The brave man blessed himself, and the boards crossing,
    bade the porter up rise, who before the prince kneeling
    gave him 'Good day, Sir Gawain!', and 'God save you!'
    Then he went on his way with the one man only
    to guide him as he goes to that grievous place
    where he is due to endure the dolorous blow.
    They go by banks and by braes where branches are bare,
    they climb along cliffs where clingeth the cold;
    the heavens are lifted high, but under them evilly
    mist hangs moist on the moor, melts on the mountains;
    every hill has a hat, a mist-mantle huge.
    Brooks break and boil on braes all about,
    bright bubbling on their banks where they bustle downwards.
    Very wild through the wood is the way they must take,
    until soon comes the season when the sun rises
          that day.
     On a high hill they abode,
     white snow beside them lay;

the man that by him rode
there bade his master stay.

84 'For so far I have taken you, sir, at this time,
and now you are near to that noted place
that you have enquired and questioned so curiously after.
But I will announce now the truth, since you are known

to me,
and you are a lord in this life that I love greatly,
if you would follow my advice you would fare better.
The place that you pass to, men perilous hold it,
the worst wight in the world in that waste dwelleth;
for he is stout and stern, and to strike he delights,
and he mightier than any man upon middle-earth is,
and his body is bigger than the four best men
that are in Arthur's house, either Hestor or others.
All goes as he chooses at the Green Chapel;
no one passes by that place so proud in his arms
that he hews not to death by dint of his hand.
For he is a man monstrous, and mercy he knows not;
for be it a churl or a chaplain that by the Chapel rideth,
a monk or a mass-priest or any man besides,
he would as soon have him slain as himself go alive.
And so I say to you, as sure as you sit in your saddle,
if you come there, you'll be killed, if the carl has his way.
Trust me, that is true, though you had twenty lives
to yield.
He here has dwelt now long
and stirred much strife on field;
against his strokes so strong
yourself you cannot shield.

85 And so, good Sir Gawain, now go another way,
     and let the man alone, for the love of God, sir!
     Come to some other country, and there may Christ keep
                            you!
     And I shall haste me home again, and on my honour I
                           promise
     that I swear will by God and all His gracious saints,
     so help me God and the Halidom, and other oaths a plenty,
     that I will safe keep your secret, and say not a word
     that ever you fain were to flee for any foe that I knew of.'
     'Gramercy!' quoth Gawain, and regretfully answered:
     'Well, man, I wish thee, who wishest my good,
     and keep safe my secret, I am certain thou wouldst.
     But however heedfully thou hid it, if I here departed
     fain in fear now to flee, in the fashion thou speakest,
     I should a knight coward be, I could not be excused.
     Nay, I'll fare to the Chapel, whatever chance may befall,
     and have such words with that wild man as my wish is
     to say, come fair or come foul, as fate will allot
         me there.
       He may be a fearsome knave
       to tame, and club may bear;
       but His servants true to save
       the Lord can well prepare.'

86 'Marry!' quoth the other man, 'now thou makest it so clear
     that thou wishest thine own bane to bring on thyself,
     and to lose thy life hast a liking, to delay thee I care not!
     Have here thy helm on thy head, thy spear in thy hand,
     and ride down by yon rock-side where runs this same track,
     till thou art brought to the bottom of the baleful valley.
     A little to thy left hand then look o'er the green,

and thou wilt see on the slope the selfsame chapel,
and the great man and grim on ground that it keeps.
Now farewell in God's name, Gawain the noble!
For all the gold in the world I would not go with thee,
nor bear thee fellowship through this forest one foot
further!'
With that his bridle towards the wood back the man turneth,
hits his horse with his heels as hard as he can,
gallops on the greenway, and the good knight there leaves
      alone,
    Quoth Gawain: 'By God on high
    I will neither grieve nor groan.
    With God's will I comply,
    Whose protection I do own.'

87 Then he put spurs to Gringolet, and espying the track,
thrust in along a bank by a thicket's border,
rode down the rough brae right to the valley;
and then he gazed all about: a grim place he thought it,
and saw no sign of shelter on any side at all,
only high hillsides sheer upon either hand,
and notched knuckled crags with gnarled boulders;
the very skies by the peaks were scraped, it appeared.
Then he halted and held in his horse for the time,
and changed oft his front the Chapel to find.
Such on no side he saw, as seemed to him strange,
save a mound as it might be near the marge of a green,
a worn barrow on a brae by the brink of a water,
beside falls in a flood that was flowing down;
the burn bubbled therein, as if boiling it were.
He urged on his horse then, and came up to the mound,
there lightly alit, and lashed to a tree
his reins, with a rough branch rightly secured them.

Then he went to the barrow and about it he walked,
debating in his mind what might the thing be.
It had a hole at the end and at either side,
and with grass in green patches was grown all over,
and was all hollow within: nought but an old cavern,
or a cleft in an old crag; he could not it name
      aright.
  'Can this be the Chapel Green,
  O Lord?' said the gentle knight.
  'Here the Devil might say, I ween,
  his matins about midnight!'

88 'On my word,' quoth Wawain, ''tis a wilderness here!
This oratory looks evil. With herbs overgrown
it fits well that fellow transformed into green
to follow here his devotions in the Devil's fashion.
Now I feel in my five wits the Fiend 'tis himself
that has trapped me with this tryst to destroy me here.
This is a chapel of mischance, the church most accursed
that ever I entered. Evil betide it!'
With high helm on his head, his lance in his hand,
he roams up to the roof of that rough dwelling.
Then he heard from the high hill, in a hard rock-wall
beyond the stream on a steep, a sudden startling noise.
How it clattered in the cliff, as if to cleave it asunder,
as if one upon a grindstone were grinding a scythe!
How it whirred and it rasped as water in a mill-race!
How it rushed, and it rang, rueful to harken!
Then 'By God,' quoth Gawain, 'I guess this ado
is meant for my honour, meetly to hail me
      as knight!
  As God wills! Waylaway!
  That helps me not a mite.

My life though down I lay,
no noise can me affright.'

89 Then clearly the knight there called out aloud:
'Who is master in this place to meet me at tryst?
For now 'tis good Gawain on ground that here walks.
If any aught hath to ask, let him hasten to me,
either now or else never, his needs to further!'
'Stay!' said one standing above on the steep o'er his head,
'and thou shalt get in good time what to give thee I vowed.'
Still with that rasping and racket he rushed on a while,
and went back to his whetting, till he wished to descend.
And then he climbed past a crag, and came from a hole,
hurtling out of a hid nook with a horrible weapon:
a Danish axe newly dressed the dint to return,
with cruel cutting-edge curved along the handle –
filed on a whetstone, and four feet in width,
'twas no less – along its lace of luminous hue;
and the great man in green still guised as before,
his locks and long beard, his legs and his face,
save that firm on his feet he fared on the ground,
steadied the haft on the stones and stalked beside it.
When he walked to the water, where he wade would not,
he hopped over on his axe and haughtily strode,
fierce and fell on a field where far all about
          lay snow.
    Sir Gawain the man met there,
    neither bent nor bowed he low.
    The other said: 'Now, sirrah fair,
    I true at tryst thee know!'

90 'Gawain,' said that green man, 'may God keep thee!
On my word, sir, I welcome thee with a will to my place,

and thou hast timed thy travels as trusty man should,
and thou hast forgot not the engagement agreed on
                                    between us:
at this time gone a twelvemonth thou took'st thy allowance,
and I should now this New Year nimbly repay thee.
And we are in this valley now verily on our own,
there are no people to part us – we can play as we like.
Have thy helm off thy head, and have here thy pay!
Bandy me no more debate than I brought before thee
when thou didst sweep off my head with one swipe only!'
'Nay', quoth Gawain, 'by God that gave me my soul,
I shall grudge thee not a grain any grief that follows.
Only restrain thee to one stroke, and still shall I stand
and offer thee no hindrance to act as thou likest
          right here.'
     With a nod of his neck he bowed,
     let bare the flesh appear;
     he would not by dread be cowed,
     no sign he gave of fear.

91 Then the great man in green gladly prepared him,
    gathered up his grim tool there Gawain to smite;
    with all the lust in his limbs aloft he heaved it,
    shaped as mighty a stroke as if he meant to destroy him.
    Had it driving come down as dour as he aimed it,
    under his dint would have died the most doughty man ever.
    But Gawain on that guisarm then glanced to one side,
    as down it came gliding on the green there to end him,
    and he shrank a little with his shoulders at the sharp iron.
    With a jolt the other man jerked back the blade,
    and reproved then the prince, proudly him taunting.
    'Thou'rt not Gawain,' said the green man, 'who is so good
                                    reported,

who never flinched from any foes on fell or in dale;
and now thou fleest in fear, ere thou feelest a hurt!
Of such cowardice that knight I ne'er heard accused.
Neither blenched I nor backed, when thy blow, sir, thou
                                                    aimedst,
nor uttered any cavil in the court of King Arthur.
My head flew to my feet, and yet fled I never;
but thou, ere thou hast any hurt, in thy heart quailest,
and so the nobler knight to be named I deserve
        therefore.'
    'I blenched once,' Gawain said,
    'and I will do so no more.
    But if on floor now falls my head,
    I cannot it restore.

92 But get busy, I beg, sir, and bring me to the point.
    Deal me my destiny, and do it out of hand!
    For I shall stand from thee a stroke and stir not again
    till thine axe hath hit me, have here my word on't!'
    'Have at thee then!' said the other, and heaved it aloft,
    and wratched him as wrathfully as if he were wild with rage.
    He made at him a mighty aim, but the man he touched not,
    holding back hastily his hand, ere hurt it might do.
    Gawain warily awaited it, and winced with no limb,
    but stood as still as a stone or the stump of a tree
    that with a hundred ravelled roots in rocks is embedded.
    This time merrily remarked then the man in the green:
    'So, now thou hast thy heart whole, a hit I must make.
    May the high order now keep thee that Arthur gave thee,
    and guard thy gullet at this go, if it can gain thee that.'
    Angrily with ire then answered Sir Gawain:
    'Why! lash away, thou lusty man! Too long dost thou
                                                    threaten.

'Tis thy heart methinks in thee that now quaileth!'
'In faith,' said the fellow, 'so fiercely thou speakest,
I no longer will linger delaying thy errand
      right now.'
   Then to strike he took his stance
   and grimaced with lip and brow.
   He that of rescue saw no chance
   was little pleased, I trow.

93 Lightly his weapon he lifted, and let it down neatly
with the bent horn of the blade towards the neck that was
                          bare;
though he hewed with a hammer-swing, he hurt him no
                          more
than to snick him on one side and sever the skin.
Through the fair fat sank the edge, and the flesh entered,
so that the shining blood o'er his shoulders was shed on
                          the earth;
and when the good knight saw the gore that gleamed on
                          the snow,
he sprang out with spurning feet a spear's length and more,
in haste caught his helm and on his head cast it,
under his fair shield he shot with a shake of his shoulders,
brandished his bright sword, and boldly he spake –
never since he as manchild of his mother was born
was he ever on this earth half so happy a man:
'Have done, sir, with thy dints! Now deal me no more!
I have stood from thee a stroke without strife on this spot,
and if thou offerest me others, I shall answer thee promptly,
and give as good again, and as grim, be assured,
      shall pay.
   But one stroke here's my due,
   as the covenant clear did say

that in Arthur's halls we drew.
And so, good sir, now stay!'

94 From him the other stood off, and on his axe rested,
held the haft to the ground, and on the head leaning,
gazed at the good knight as on the green he there strode.
To see him standing so stout, so stern there and fearless,
armed and unafraid, his heart it well pleased.
Then merrily he spoke with a mighty voice,
and loudly it rang, as to that lord he said:
'Fearless knight on this field, so fierce do not be!
No man here unmannerly hath thee maltreated,
nor aught given thee not granted by agreement at court.
A hack I thee vowed, and thou'st had it, so hold thee
content;
I remit thee the remnant of all rights I might claim.
If I brisker had been, a buffet, it may be,
I could have handed thee more harshly, and harm could
have done thee.
First I menaced thee in play with no more than a trial,
and clove thee with no cleft: I had a claim to the feint,
for the fast pact we affirmed on the first evening,
and thou fairly and unfailing didst faith with me keep,
all thy gains thou me gavest, as good man ought.
The other trial for the morning, man, I thee tendered
when thou kissedst my comely wife, and the kisses didst
render.
For the two here I offered only two harmless feints
to make.
The true shall truly repay,
for no peril then need he quake.
Thou didst fail on the third day,
and so that tap now take!

95 For it is my weed that thou wearest, that very woven girdle:
   my own wife it awarded thee, I wot well indeed.
   Now I am aware of thy kisses, and thy courteous ways,
   and of thy wooing by my wife: I worked that myself!
   I sent her to test thee, and thou seem'st to me truly
   the fair knight most faultless that e'er foot set on earth!
   As a pearl than white pease is prized more highly,
   so is Gawain, in good faith, than other gallant knights.
   But in this you lacked, sir, a little, and of loyalty came short.
   But that was for no artful wickedness, nor for wooing either,
   but because you loved your own life: the less do I blame
                                                         you.'

The other stern knight in a study then stood a long while,
in such grief and disgust he had a grue in his heart;
all the blood from his breast in his blush mingled,
and he shrank into himself with shame at that speech.
The first words on that field that he found then to say
were: 'Cursed be ye, Coveting, and Cowardice also!
In you is vileness, and vice that virtue destroyeth.'
He took then the treacherous thing, and untying the knot
fiercely flung he the belt at the feet of the knight:
'See there the falsifier, and foul be its fate!
Through care for thy blow Cowardice brought me
to consent to Coveting, my true kind to forsake,
which is free-hand and faithful word that are fitting to
                                                      knights.

Now I am faulty and false, who afraid have been ever
of treachery and troth-breach: the two now my curse
          may bear!
     I confess, sir, here to you
     all faulty has been my fare.
     Let me gain your grace anew,
     and after I will beware.'

96   Then the other man laughed and lightly answered:
    'I hold it healed beyond doubt, the harm that I had.
    Thou hast confessed thee so clean and acknowledged thine
                                             errors,
    and hast the penance plain to see from the point of
    my blade,
    that I hold thee purged of that debt, made as pure and as
                                             clean
    as hadst thou done no ill deed since the day thou wert born.
    And I give thee, sir, the girdle with gold at its hems,
    for it is green like my gown. So, Sir Gawain, you may
    think of this our contest when in the throng thou walkest
    among princes of high praise; 'twill be a plain reminder
    of the chance of the Green Chapel between chivalrous
                                           knights.
    And now you shall in this New Year come anon to my house,
    and in our revels the rest of this rich season
        shall go.'
      The lord pressed him hard to wend,
      and said, 'my wife, I know,
      we soon shall make your friend,
      who was your bitter foe.'

97   'Nay forsooth!' the knight said, and seized then his helm,
    and duly it doffed, and the doughty man thanked:
    'I have lingered too long! May your life now be blest,
    and He promptly repay you Who apportions all honours!
    And give my regards to her grace, your goodly consort,
    both to her and to the other, to mine honoured ladies,
    who thus their servant with their designs have subtly
                                          beguiled.
    But no marvel it is if mad be a fool,
    and by the wiles of woman to woe be brought.

For even so Adam by one on earth was beguiled,
and Solomon by several, and to Samson moreover
his doom by Delilah was dealt; and David was after
blinded by Bathsheba, and he bitterly suffered.
Now if these came to grief through their guile, a gain
                                'twould be vast
to love them well and believe them not, if it lay in man's
                                    power!
Since these were aforetime the fairest, by fortune most blest,
eminent among all the others who under heaven bemused
     were too,
   and all of them were betrayed
   by women that they knew,
   though a fool I now am made,
   some excuse I think my due.'

98 'But for your girdle,' quoth Gawain, 'may God you repay!
That I will gain with good will, not for the gold so joyous
of the cincture, nor the silk, nor the swinging pendants,
nor for wealth, nor for worth, nor for workmanship fine;
but as a token of my trespass I shall turn to it often
when I ride in renown, ruefully recalling
the failure and the frailty of the flesh so perverse,
so tender, so ready to take taints of defilement.
And thus, when pride my heart pricks for prowess in arms,
one look at this love-lace shall lowlier make it.
But one thing I would pray you, if it displeaseth you not,
since you are the lord of yonder land, where I lodged for a
                                    while
in your house and in honour – may He you reward
Who upholdeth the heavens and on high sitteth! –
how do you announce your true name? And then nothing
                                    further.'

'That I will tell thee truly,' then returned the other.
'Bertilak de Hautdesert hereabouts I am called,
[who thus have been enchanted and changed in my hue]
by the might of Morgan le Fay that in my mansion dwelleth,
and by cunning of lore and crafts well learned.
The magic arts of Merlin she many hath mastered;
for deeply in dear love she dealt on a time
with that accomplished clerk, as at Camelot runs
      the fame;
   and Morgan the Goddess
   is therefore now her name.
   None power and pride possess
   too high for her to tame.

99 She made me go in this guise to your goodly court
to put its pride to the proof, if the report were true
that runs of the great renown of the Round Table.
She put this magic upon me to deprive you of your wits,
in hope Guinevere to hurt, that she in horror might die
aghast at that glamoury that gruesomely spake
with its head in its hand before the high table.
She it is that is at home, that ancient lady;
she is indeed thine own aunt, Arthur's half-sister,
daughter of the Duchess of Tintagel on whom doughty Sir
                         Uther
after begat Arthur, who in honour is now.
Therefore I urge thee in earnest, sir, to thine aunt return!
In my hall make merry! My household thee loveth,
and I wish thee as well, upon my word, sir knight,
as any that go under God, for thy great loyalty.'
But he denied him with a 'Nay! by no means I will!'
They clasp then and kiss and to the care give each other

of the Prince of Paradise; and they part on that field
      so cold,
  To the king's court on courser keen
  then hastened Gawain the bold,
  and the knight in the glittering green
  to ways of his own did hold.

100 Wild ways in the world Wawain now rideth
on Gringolet: by the grace of God he still lived.
Oft in house he was harboured and lay oft in the open,
oft vanquished his foe in adventures as he fared
which I intend not this time in my tale to recount.
The hurt was healed that he had in his neck,
and the bright-hued belt he bore now about it
obliquely like a baldric bound at his side,
under his left arm with a knot that lace was fastened
to betoken he had been detected in the taint of a fault;
and so at last he came to the Court again safely.
Delight there was awakened, when the lords were aware
that good Gawain had returned: glad news they thought it.
The king kissed the knight, and the queen also,
and then in turn many a true knight that attended to greet
                      him.
About his quest they enquire, and he recounts all the
                        marvels,
declares all the hardships and care that he had,
what chanced at the Chapel, what cheer made the knight,
the love of the lady, and the lace at the last.
The notch in his neck naked he showed them
that he had for his dishonesty from the hands of the
      knight in blame.
  It was torment to tell the truth:

in his face the blood did flame;
he groaned for grief and ruth
when he showed it, to his shame.

101 'Lo! Lord,' he said at last, and the lace handled,
'This is the band! For this a rebuke I bear in my neck!
This is the grief and disgrace I have got for myself
from the covetousness and cowardice that o'ercame me
there!
This is the token of the troth-breach that I am detected in,
and needs must I wear it while in the world I remain;
for a man may cover his blemish, but unbind it he cannot,
for where once 'tis applied, thence part will it never.'
The king comforted the knight, and all the Court also
laughed loudly thereat, and this law made in mirth
the lords and the ladies that whoso belonged to the Table,
every knight of the Brotherhood, a baldric should have,
a band of bright green obliquely about him,
and this for love of that knight as a livery should wear.
For that was reckoned the distinction of the Round Table,
and honour was his that had it evermore after,
as it is written in the best of the books of romance.
Thus in Arthur his days happened this marvel,
as the Book of the Brut beareth us witness;
since Brutus the bold knight to Britain came first,
after the siege and the assault had ceased at Troy,
I trow,
many a marvel such before,
has happened here ere now.
To His bliss us bring Who bore
the Crown of Thorns on brow!   AMEN

HONY SOYT QUI MAL PENCE

W.P. KER MEMORIAL LECTURE
ON *SIR GAWAIN*

It is a great honour to be invited to lecture in this ancient university, and under the illustrious name of W. P. Ker. I was once allowed to use for a time his copy of *Sir Gawain and the Green Knight*. It showed clearly that he had – as usual, in spite of the enormous range of his reading and experience of literature – read this work with close attention.

It is indeed a poem that deserves close and detailed attention, and after that (not before, according to a too common critical procedure) careful consideration, and re-consideration. It is one of the masterpieces of fourteenth-century art in England, and of English Literature as a whole. It is one of those greater works which not only bear the trampling of the Schools, endure becoming a *text*, indeed (severest test) a *set text*, but yield more and more under this pressure. For it belongs to that literary kind which has deep roots in the past, deeper even than its author was aware. It is made of tales often told before and elsewhere, and of elements that derive from remote times, beyond the vision or awareness of the poet: like *Beowulf*, or some of Shakespeare's major plays, such as *King Lear* or *Hamlet*.

It is an interesting question: what is this flavour, this atmosphere, this virtue that such *rooted* works have, and which compensates for the inevitable flaws and imperfect adjustments that must appear, when plots, motives, symbols, are rehandled and pressed into the service of the changed minds of a later time, used for the expression of ideas quite different from those which produced them. But though *Sir Gawain* would be a very suitable text on which to base a discussion of this question, that is not the kind of thing about which I wish to speak today. I am not concerned at this moment with research into the origins of the tale or its details, or into the question of precisely in what form these reached the author of this poem, before he set to work on it. I wish to speak about his handling of the matter, or one particular aspect of this: the movement of his mind, as he wrote and (I do not doubt) re-wrote the story, until it had the form that has come down to us. But the other question must not be forgotten. Antiquity like a many-figured back-cloth hangs ever behind the scene. Behind our poem stalk the figures of elder myth, and through the lines are heard the echoes of ancient cults, beliefs and symbols remote from the consciousness of an educated moralist (but also a poet) of the late fourteenth century. His story is not *about* those old things, but it receives part of its life, its vividness, its tension from them. That is the way with the greater fairy-stories — of which this is one. There is indeed no better medium for moral teaching than the good fairy-story (by which I mean a real deep-rooted tale, told as a tale, and not a thinly disguised moral allegory). As the author of *Sir Gawain*, it would seem, perceived; or felt instinctively, rather than consciously: for being a man of the fourteenth century, a serious, didactic, encyclopaedic, not to say pedantic century, he inherited 'faerie', rather than turned deliberately to it.

Out of all the many new things, then, upon which one might hope to say something new — even now, when this poem has become the subject of several editions, translations, discussions, and numerous articles – such as the Beheading Game, the Perilous Host, the Green Man, the Sunlike mythical figure that looms behind the courteous Gawain, nephew of King Arthur, as certainly if more remotely as the Bear-boy lurks behind the heroic Beowulf, nephew of King Hygelac; or such as the Irish influence on Britain, and the influence of both on France, and the French return; or coming down to our author's own time: the 'Alliterative Revival', and the contemporary debate about its use in narrative, almost lost now save for brief echoes in *Sir Gawain* and in Chaucer (who, I think, knew *Sir Gawain*, and probably the author also) – out of all these and other matters which the title *Sir Gawain and the Green Knight* might suggest I wish to turn to one, more neglected, and yet, I think, more fundamentally important: the kernel, the very nub of the poem as it was finally made, its great third 'fit', and within that the temptation of Sir Gawain and his confession.

In speaking of this matter, the temptation and confession of Gawain, I must rely, of course, on a knowledge of the poem as a whole, in itself or in a translation. Where quotation is essential, I will use a translation which I have just completed, since I have made it with two objects (to some extent, I hope, achieved): to preserve the original metre and alliteration, without which translation is of little value except as a crib; and to preserve, to exhibit in an intelligible modern idiom, the nobility and the courtesy of this poem, by a poet to whom 'courtesy' meant so much.

Since I am not speaking of the poem as a whole, or its admirable construction, I need only indicate one point in this, which is for my purpose significant. The poem is divided into four fits or cantos; but the third is much the largest, much more than a quarter of the whole (872 lines out of a total of 2530): a numerical pointer, as it were, to the real primary interest of the poet. And yet actually he has tried to conceal the numerical evidence by attaching, skilfully yet artificially, part of what really belongs to the situation of the Third Fit to the Second Fit. The temptation of Sir Gawain really begins as far back as the beginning of stanza 39 (line 928) (if not earlier) and lasts for more than a thousand lines. All else is by comparison, even when highly pictorial, perfunctory. The temptation was to this poet the raison d'être of his poem; all else was to him scenery, background, or else machinery: a device for getting Sir Gawain into the situation which he wished to study.

Of what lay before, therefore, I need only briefly remind you. We have the setting, with a brief sketch of the magnificence of the Arthurian court in the midst of the highest festival of the year (to the English), the feast of Christmas. At dinner on New Year's Day there rides into the hall a great Green Knight on a green horse, with a green axe, and issues his challenge: any man in the court that has the courage may take the axe and strike the Green Knight a single unopposed blow, on condition that he promises after a year and a day to allow the Green Knight to give him one unopposed blow in return.

In the event it is Sir Gawain that takes up the challenge. But of all this I wish only to point out one important aspect. From this very beginning we can already perceive the moral purpose of the poet at work, or we can do so at a re-reading, after consideration. It is necessary to the temptation that Gawain's actions should be capable of moral approbation; and amidst all the 'faerie' the poet is at pains to show that they were so. He takes up the challenge to rescue the king from the false position in which his rashness has placed him. Gawain's motive is not pride in his own prowess, not boastfulness, not even the light-hearted frivolity of knights making absurd bets and vows in the midst of the Christmas revels. His motive is a humble one: the protection of Arthur, his elder kinsman, of his king, of the head of the Round Table, from indignity and peril, and the risking instead of himself, the least of the knights (as he declares), and the one whose loss could most easily be endured. He is involved therefore in the business, as far as it was possible to make the fairy-story go, as a matter of duty and humility and self-sacrifice. And since the absurdity of the challenge could not wholly be got rid of – absurdity, that is, if the story is to be conducted on a serious moral plane, in which every action of the hero, Gawain, is to be scrutinized and morally assessed – the king himself is criticized, both by the author as narrator, and by the lords of the court.

One further point, to which we shall return later. From the beginning Gawain is tricked, or at least trapped. He accepts the challenge, to deal the blow *quat-so bifallez after* ('whatever the consequences') and in a year's time to present himself, without substitute or assistant, to receive a return blow with whatever weapon the Green Knight chooses. He is no sooner involved than he is informed that he must seek out the Green Knight himself, to get his 'wages' where he lives in some region unnamed. He accepts this onerous addition. But when he had delivered the stroke and beheaded the Knight, the trap is sprung; for the challenger is not slain, he picks up his own head, strides back onto his horse, and rides off, after the ugly severed head, held aloft in his hand, has warned Gawain to be true to his vow.

Now we, and no doubt many of our poet's audience, may not be surprised by this. If we are introduced to a green man, with green hair and face, on a green horse, at the court of King Arthur, we expect 'magic'; and Arthur and Gawain should have expected it also, we think. As indeed most of those present seem to have done: 'a phantom and fay-magic folk there thought it' (11.240). But this poet was as it were determined to take the story and its machinery for granted, and then examine the problems of conduct, especially as regards Sir Gawain, that arose. One of the things that he will be most concerned with is *lewté*, 'keeping faith'. It is therefore highly important from the outset to consider precisely the relations of the Green Knight and Gawain, and the exact nature of the contract between them, just as if we were dealing with a normal and possible engagement between two 'gentlemen'. Thus the poet is at pains, I think, to indicate that the 'magic', though it might be feared as a possibility by the challenged, is concealed by the challenger in the drawing up of the agreement. The king takes the challenge at its face-value, a piece of folly: that is, asking to be slain on the spot; and later, when Gawain is preparing his blow:

'Take care, cousin,' quoth the king, 'one cut to address,
and if thou learnest him his lesson, I believe very well
that thou wilt bear any blow that he gives back later.'

(17.372–4)

And so, though Gawain's good faith is involved – by his own words: *quat-so bifallez after* – his opponent has actually concealed the fact that he could not be slain in this manner, being protected by magic. And Gawain is now pledged to a perilous quest and journey the only probable end of which will be his death. For he has not (yet) any magic; and when the time comes he must set forth, the deliverer of his king and kinsman, and the upholder of the honour of his order, with unflinching courage and *lewté*, alone and unprotected.

The time does come at last, and Sir Gawain prepares to

depart in search of the Green Knight and the Green Chapel where the tryst has been set. And then at least the poet allows no room for doubt, whatever you may think of my intro-duction of ethical considerations into the First Fit, and the fairy-tale scene of the Beheading. He describes the armour of Sir Gawain, and though we now may be caught rather by the contrast of his glowing scarlet and glittering gold with the green of the challenger, and ponder its possible inherited significance, the poet's interest is not there. He gives in fact all told only a few lines to all the gear and the colour red (*red* and *goulez*) is only twice named. It is the shield with which he is concerned. The shield of Gawain he uses indeed to bla-zon forth his own mind and purpose, and to that he devotes three whole stanzas. Upon the shield he imposes – and we may deliberately use this word, for here beyond doubt we have an addition of his own – instead of the heraldic charges found in other romances, lion, eagle, or gryphon, the symbol of the pentangle. Now it does not greatly matter what sig-nificance or significances are elsewhere or earlier ascribed to this symbol.[1] Just as it does not matter greatly what other or older significances were attached to green or red, to holly or to axes. For the significance that the pentangle is to bear in this poem is made plain – plain enough, that is, in general purport[2]: it is to betoken 'perfection' indeed, but perfection in religion (the Christian faith), in piety and morality, and the 'courtesy' that flows therefrom into human relations; perfection in the details of each, and a perfect and unbro-ken bond between the higher and lower planes. It is with this sign upon his shield (and as we later learn embroidered also on his coat-armour), imposed there by our poet (for the reasons that he gives for the use of it are in themselves and in the style of their enumeration such as Sir Gawain himself could not possibly have had, still less openly asserted, for the adoption of this charge) – it is with this sign that Sir Gawain rides forth from Camelot.

His long and perilous journey in search of the Green Chapel is briefly, and in general adequately described. Adequately, that is, if in places perfunctory, and in others obscure to the commentators, for the purpose of the poet. He is anxious now to reach the castle of the temptation. We need not concern ourselves on this occasion with any further points until the castle comes in sight. And when it does, we shall be concerned with what the author has made of it, not with the materials, wholly different in purport, out of which he may be thought to have built it.

How does Gawain find the castle? *In answer to prayer.* He has been journeying since All Hallows. It is now Christmas Eve, and he is lost in a wild strange country of tangled forest; but his chief concern is that he should not miss Mass on Christmas morning. He was

> troubled lest a truant at that time he should prove
> from the service of the sweet Lord, who on that selfsame
> night
> of a maid became man our mourning to conquer.
> And therefore sighing he said: 'I beseech thee, O Lord,
> and Mary who is the mildest mother most dear,
> for some harbour where with honour I might hear the Mass
> and thy Matins tomorrow. This meekly I ask,
> and thereto promptly I pray with Pater and Ave and Creed.'
>
> (32.750–8)

It is when he has so prayed, and made an act of contrition, and blessed himself thrice with the sign of the cross, that he suddenly catches sight through the trees of the beautiful white castle, and rides on to a courteous welcome, and the answer to his prayer.

Out of whatever more ancient stones may have been built the gleaming but solid magnificence of this castle, whatever turn the story may take, whatever details may be discovered that the author inherited and overlooked or failed to accommodate to his new purpose, this much is clear: our poet is bringing Gawain to no haunt of demons, enemies of human kind, but to a courteous and Christian hall. There the Court of Arthur and the Round Table are held in honour; and there the chapel-bells ring for Vespers, and the kind air of Christendom blows.

> On the morn when every man remembers the time
> that our dear Lord for our doom to die was born,
> in every home wakes happiness on earth for His sake.
> So did it there on that day with the dearest delights.
>
> (41.995–8)

There Gawain was to feel and be 'at home' for a short while, to find himself unexpectedly in the midst of the life and society that he most liked, and where his very skill and pleasure in courteous converse would ensure him the highest honour.

Yet his temptation has begun. We shall not appreciate it at a first reading perhaps, but any reconsideration will reveal it to us that this strange tale, this *mayn meruayle* (whether we believe in it or not), has been carefully re-drawn by a skilled hand directed by a wise and noble mind. It is in the very setting to which Gawain is used, and in which he has hitherto achieved the highest repute, that he is to be tested, within Christendom and so as a Christian. He himself and all that he stands for are to be assayed.

And if the pentangle with its touch of learned pedantry, at war it seemed with the artistic instinct of a narrative poet,[3] may for a moment have made us fear that we were going to lose Faerie only to gain a formalized allegory, we are now swiftly reassured. 'Perfection' Gawain may have been given as a standard to strive for (for with no less ideal could he achieve a near-perfection), but he himself is not presented as a mathematical allegory, but as a man, an individual human being. His very 'courtesy' proceeds not solely from the ideals, or the fashions, of his imagined time, but from his own character. He enjoys the sweet society of gentle ladies intensely, and he is immediately moved deeply by beauty. This is how his first meeting with the fair Lady of the Castle is described. Gawain had attended Vespers in the chapel, and when they are over the lady comes forth from her private pew.

> And from her closet she came with many comely maidens.
> She was fairer in face, in her flesh and her skin,
> her proportions, her complexion, and her port than all
>   others,
> and more lovely than Guinevere to Gawain she looked.
> He came through the chancel to pay court to her grace ...
>
> (39.942–6)

There follows a brief description of her beauty in contrast to the old and wrinkled and ugly lady that was at her side:

> For if the younger was youthful, yellow was the elder;
> with rose-hue the one face was richly mantled,
> rough wrinkled cheeks rolled on the other;
> on the kerchiefs of the one many clear pearls were,
> her breast and bright throat were bare displayed,
> fairer than white snow that falls on the hills;

the other was clad with a cloth that enclosed all her neck,
enveloped was her black chin with chalk-white veils ...

(39.951–8)

When Gawain glimpsed that gay lady that so gracious
   looked,
with leave sought of the lord towards the ladies he went;
the elder he saluted, low to her bowing,
about the lovelier he laid then lightly his arms
and kissed her in courtly wise with courtesy speaking.

(40.970–4)

And the next day at the dinner on Christmas Day he is set
on the dais beside her, and of all the mirth and splendour of
the feast the author (as he says himself) is concerned only to
depict their delight.

Yet I ween that Wawain and that woman so fair
in companionship took such pleasure together
in sweet society soft words speaking,
their courteous converse clean and clear of all evil,
that with their pleasant pastime no prince's sport
     compares.
   Drums beat, and trumps men wind,
   many pipers play their airs;
   each man his needs did mind,
   and they two minded theirs.   (41.1010–19)

This is the setting, but the situation is not yet fully prepared.
Though Gawain takes his ease for a while, he does not forget
his quest. For four days he enjoys the merrymaking, but in
the evening of the fourth day when there are now but three
left of the old year before the appointed New Year's Day,

he begs leave to depart on the morrow. He tells no more of his errand than that he is obliged to try and find a place called the Green Chapel and reach it on New Year's morning. Then he is told by the lord that he can rest at ease three days longer and complete the cure of all the hardships of his journey, for the Green Chapel is not two miles away. A guide shall be found to lead him thither on the morning itself.

At this point the author makes one of his many skilful combinations of elements of older fairy-story with the character of Gawain (as he is depicting him) to provide the machinery of his own version. In what follows we glimpse the Perilous Host who must be obeyed in every command, however silly or outrageous it may seem; but we see also that warmth, almost we might say impetuous excess, of courtesy that characterizes Gawain. Just as when he rehearsed the compact with the Green Knight he said largely 'whatever may be the consequences' and so landed himself in more than he bargained for; so now in delight and gratitude he cries:

'Now I thank you a thousand times for this beyond all!
Now my quest is accomplished, as you crave it, I will
dwell a few days here, and else do what you order.'

(44.1080–2)

The lord immediately seizes on this, and holds him to his word: Gawain is to lie late abed, and then spend the days with the lady, while the lord goes off hunting. And then a seemingly absurd compact is propounded.

'One thing more,' said the master, 'we'll make an agreement:
whatever I win in the wood at once shall be yours,
and whatever gain you may get you shall give in exchange.

Shall we swap thus, sweet man – come, say what you think! –
whether one's luck be light, or one's lot be better?'
'By God,' quoth good Gawain, 'I agree to it all,
and whatever play you propose seems pleasant to me.'
'Done! 'Tis a bargain! Who'll bring us the drink?'
So said the lord of that land. They laughed one and all;
they drank and they dallied, and they did as they pleased,
these lords and ladies, as long as they wished,
and then with customs of France and many courtly phrases
they stood in sweet debate and soft words bandied,
and lovingly they kissed, their leave taking.
With trusty attendants and torches gleaming
they were brought at the last to their beds so soft,
      one and all.
    Yet ere to bed they came,
    he the bargain did oft recall;
    he knew how to play a game
    the old governor of that hall.   (45.1105–25)

So ends the Second Fit and the great Third Fit begins,
about which I wish specially to speak. I will say little about
its admirable construction, since that has often been com-
mented upon. Indeed (once granted an interest in contem-
porary sport and its details, or even without that concession)
its excellence is obvious enough to any attentive reader: the
way in which the hunts are 'interleaved' between the tempta-
tions; the significant diminuendo from the herds of deer (of
real economic value in winter) slain in the first hunt to the
'foul fox-fell' of the last day, contrasting with the increasing
peril of the temptations; the dramatic purpose of the hunts,
not only in timing, and in preserving a double view with
the three main actors kept all the while in sight, but also in
elongating and making most weighty the three vital days out

of the whole year of the general action: all this needs no elaboration.[4] But the hunts have also another function, essential to the handling of the tale in this version, that is more to my purpose. As I have already indicated, any consideration of 'analogues', especially the less courtly, or indeed any close examination of our text without reference to others, will suggest that our poet has done his best to turn the place of the temptation into a real chivalrous castle, no mirage of enchantment or abode of fays, where the laws of courtesy, hospitality, and morality run. The hunts play a significant place in this change of atmosphere. The lord behaves as a real wealthy lord might be expected to behave in the season. He must be out of the way, but he does not remain mysteriously aloof, or just vanish. His absence and the lady's opportunity are thus accounted for naturally; and this helps to make the temptations also more natural, and so to set them on a normal moral plane.

There would not, I think, and I am sure that the author intended that there should not, be any more suspicion in the minds of genuine first-time readers or hearers of his story[5] than in the mind of Sir Gawain himself (as is clearly shown) that the temptations were all a 'put-up job', just part of the perils and trials that he had been inveigled from Arthur's court to undergo and so be destroyed or utterly disgraced. In fact it is possible to wonder whether the author has not gone too far. Has not his contrivance a grave weakness? All – apart perhaps from unusual but not incredible magnificence – all is so normal in the castle that on reflexion the question must soon arise: 'What would have happened, if Gawain had not passed the test?' For we learn in the end that the lord and lady were conniving; yet the test was meant to be real, to procure if possible Gawain's downfall and the disgrace of his 'high order'. The lady was in fact his 'enemy keen'. How then was she protected, if her lord was far away, hallooing and hunting in the forest? It is no answer to this question to point to ancient and barbaric customs or to tales in which memory of them is still enshrined. For we are not in that world, and if indeed the author knew anything about it he has wholly rejected it. But he has not wholly rejected 'magic'. And the answer may be that 'fairy-story', though concealed, or taken for granted as part of the machinery of events, is really as integral to this part of the narrative as to those where it is more obvious and unaltered, such as the incursion of the Green Knight. Only *fairyȝe* (240) will suffice to make the plot of the lord and lady intelligible and workable in the imagined world that the author has contrived. We must suppose that just as Sir Bertilak could go green again and change shape for the tryst at the Chapel, so the lady could have protected herself by some sudden change, or destroying power, to which Sir Gawain would have become exposed by falling to temptation, even in will only.[6] If we have this in mind, then perhaps the 'weakness' becomes strength. The temptation is real and perilous in the extreme on the *moral plane* (for Gawain's own view of the circumstances is all that matters on that plane[7]); yet hanging in the background, for those able to receive the air of 'faerie' in a romance, is a terrible threat of disaster and destruction. The struggle becomes intense to a degree which a merely realistic story of how a pious knight resisted a temptation to adultery (when a guest) could hardly attain.[8] It is one of the properties of Fairy Story thus to enlarge the scene and the actors; or rather it is one of the properties that are distilled by literary alchemy when old deep-rooted stories are rehandled by a real poet with an imagination of his own.

In my view, then, the temptations of Sir Gawain, his behaviour under them, and criticism of his code, were for our author his story, to which all else was subservient. I will not argue this. The weight, length, and detailed elaboration of the Third Fit (and of the end of the Second Fit which defines the situation) are, as I have said, sufficient evidence to show where at least the prime attention of the poet was concentrated.

I will turn then now to the temptation scenes, especially to those points in them that are most significant, as I believe, of the author's views and purpose: the keys to the question 'what is this poem really about?' as it is by him presented. For this purpose it is necessary to have fresh in mind the conversations of Gawain and the Lady of the Castle.

(Here the temptation-scenes were read aloud in translation).[9]

From these scenes I will select some points for comment. On December the 29th the lady comes to Gawain's room before he is fully awake, sits upon his bed-side, and when he arouses puts her arms about him (49.1224–5). She tells him that all is quite safe, and makes her all-out assault. It is, I think, here important to say that though some critics have held this to be a mistake on her part (which can in reality mean only a mistake on the part of the poet), they themselves are certainly mistaken. The lady is very beautiful indeed, Gawain was from the first, as we have seen, greatly attracted by her, and not only is he severely tempted on this occasion, but by the lady's declaration (49.1235–40) *that temptation remains in force throughout his dealings with her*. All their converse and talk slips perpetually towards adultery thereafter.

After the first temptation no private conversation between Gawain and the lady (except in his room) is reported – he is either with at least both the ladies together, or after the lord's homecomings in company – save only in the evening after the second temptation. And we may well consider the change that has occurred, contrasting the scene after supper on December the 30th with the untroubled air at dinner on Christmas Day (which I have already recited, p. 119):

Much gladness and gaiety began then to spring
round the fire on the hearth, and freely and oft
at supper and later: many songs of delight,
such as canticles of Christmas, and new carol-dances,
amid all the mannerly mirth that men can tell of;
and ever our noble knight was next to the lady.
Such glances she gave him of her gracious favour,
secretly stealing sweet looks that strong man to charm,
that he was passing perplexed, and ill-pleased at heart.
Yet he would fain not of his courtesy coldly refuse her,
but graciously engaged her, however against the grain
      the play.   (66.1652–63)

This I believe to be a fair translation of a passage that contains some verbal, and possibly textual, difficulties; but neither this version nor the original must be misunderstood. Gawain's mood is not that of one who has been 'put off' or disgusted, but of a man who does not know what to do. He is in the throes of temptation. All his breeding constrains him to go on playing the game, but the lady has already exposed the weakness of such 'nurture', that it is a perilous weapon in such a situation, as dangerous as a handful of pretty rockets near a real gunpowder-plot. Immediately afterwards fear or prudence suggests flight, and Gawain tries to get out of his promise to do the lord's bidding and stay three nights longer. But he is caught again by his own courtesy. He has no better excuse to offer than to say that it is very near the time for his appointment, and he had better start in the morning.

This the lord easily counters by pretending to think that his own good faith is doubted, and he repeats that he gives his word that Sir Gawain shall reach the Green Chapel in good time. That this attempt at flight on Gawain's part is due to moral wisdom (to fear of himself, that is) and not to disgust is made clear by the sequel.

Apart from this hint, however, in the first two scenes the author has been content to report events and sayings without revealing Gawain's feelings (or his own views). But as soon as we come to the third scene the tone changes. So far Gawain has been engaged mainly in a problem of 'courtesy', and we see him using the wits and good manners for which he was renowned with great skill, and still (until the evening of December the 30th) with a certain confidence. But with stanzas 70 and 71 (lines 1750 ff.) we come to the 'nub' of the affair. Gawain is now in great peril. Wise flight has proved impossible without breaking his word and the rules of courtesy to his host.[10] His sleep has been dark and troubled with the fear of death. And when the lady appears again he welcomes her with sheer pleasure and delight in her beauty. On the last morning of the old year she came again to his room:

> in a gay mantle that to the ground was measured
> and was fur-lined most fairly with fells well trimmed,
> with no comely coif on her head, only the clear jewels
> that were twined in her tressure by twenties in clusters;
> her noble face and her neck all naked were laid,
> her breast bare in front and at the back also.
> She came through the chamber-door and closed it behind
>   her,
> wide set a window, and to wake him she called,
> thus greeting him gaily with her gracious words of
>   cheer:

'Ah! man, how canst thou sleep,
the morning is so clear!'
He lay in darkness deep,
but her call he then could hear.

In heavy darkness drowsing he dream-words muttered,
as a man whose mind was bemused with many mournful
                                        thoughts,
how destiny should his doom on that day bring him
when he at the Green Chapel the great man would meet,
and be obliged his blow to abide without debate at all.
But when so comely she came, he recalled then his wits,
swept aside his slumbers, and swiftly made answer.
The lady in lovely guise came laughing sweetly,
bent down o'er his dear face, and deftly kissed him.
He greeted her graciously with a glad welcome,
seeing her so glorious and gaily attired,
so faultless in her features and so fine in her hues
that at once joy up-welling went warm to his heart.
With smiles sweet and soft they turned swiftly to mirth,
and only brightness and bliss was broached there between
        them so gay.
    They spoke then speeches good,
    much pleasure was in that play;
    great peril between them stood,
    unless Mary for her knight should pray   (69–70.1736–69)

And with that we have the re-entry, for the first time since
the pentangle and the shield of Gawain (that is here indeed
alluded to), of *religion*, of something higher than and beyond
a code of polite or polished manners which have proved, and
are going again and finally to prove, not only an ineffectual
weapon in the last resort, but an actual danger, playing into
the hands of the enemy.

Immediately afterwards the word *synne* is introduced, for the first and only time in this highly moral poem, and so all the more emphatically; and what is more, a distinction is drawn, Gawain himself is forced to draw, a distinction between 'sin' (the moral law) and 'courtesy':

For she, queenly and peerless, pressed him so closely,
led him so near the line, that at last he must needs
either refuse her with offence or her favours there take.
He cared for his courtesy, lest a caitiff[11] he proved,
yet more for his sad case, if he should sin commit
and to the owner of the house, to his host, be a traitor.
'God help me!' said he. 'Happen that shall not!'

(71.1770–6)

The end of the last temptation-scene, with the lady's complete shift of ground after her final defeat on the major (or higher, or only real) issue, is, of course, an added complexity in this complex poem, which must be considered in its place. But we must from this point move at once to the scene that follows the temptation: Gawain's confession (75.1874–84).

Gollancz at least deserves credit for noting the confession,[12] which had previously received little or no attention. But he totally missed the point, or points, involved. These I wish now specially to consider. It is not too much to say that the whole interpretation and valuation of *Sir Gawain and the Green Knight* depends on what one thinks of the thirtieth stanza of the Third Fit [stanza 75]. Either the poet knew what he was about, meant what he said, and placed this stanza where he wished it to be – in which case we must think about it seriously and consider his intentions; or else he did not, and was just a muddler, stringing conventional

scenes together, and his work is not worth long considera-
tion at all, except, perhaps, as a lumber-room of old half-for-
gotten and less than half-understood stories and motives,
just a fairy-story for adults, and not a very good one.

Gollancz evidently thought the latter; for in his notes he
makes the astonishing remark that *though the poet does not
notice it* (!), *Gawain makes a sacrilegious confession. For he con-
ceals the fact that he has accepted the girdle with the intention of
retaining it.* This is arrant nonsense. It will not even endure
reference to the text, as we shall see. But, first of all, it is quite
incredible that a poet of high seriousness[13] who has already
with explicit moral purpose inserted a long digression on
the Pentangle and the shield of Sir Gawain, should put in
a passage about *confession and absolution* (matters which he
regarded with the greatest solemnity, whatever critics may
now feel) quite casually, and without 'noticing' such a minor
point as 'sacrilege'. If he was such a fool, one wonders why
editors trouble to edit his works.

Let us look then at the text. First: since the author does
not specify what Gawain confessed, we cannot say what he
omitted, and it is therefore gratuitously silly to assert that he
concealed anything. We are told, however, that he *schewed
his mysdedez, of þe more and þe mynne*, that is, that he con-
fessed all his sins (sc. all that it was necessary to confess)
both great and small. If that is not definite enough, it is made
still plainer that Gawain's confession was a good one, and
not 'sacrilegious', and the absolution effective,[14] by the state-
ment that this was so:

There he cleanly confessed him and declared his misdeeds,
both the more and the less, and for mercy he begged,
to absolve him of them all he besought the good man;
and he assoiled him and made him as safe and as clean

129

as for Doom's Day indeed, were it due on the morrow.

(75.1880–4)

And if even this is not enough the poet goes on to describe the consequent lightness of Gawain's heart.

> Thereafter more merry he made among the fair ladies,
> with carol-dances gentle and all kinds of rejoicing,
> than ever he did ere that day, till the darkness of night,
>   in bliss.
>   Each man there said: 'I vow
>   a delight to all he is!
>   Since hither he came till now,
>   he was ne'er so gay as this.'   (75.1885–92)

Need I say that a light heart is certainly not the mood induced by a bad confession and the wilful concealment of sin?

Gawain's confession is represented as a good one, then. Yet the girdle is retained. This cannot be accidental or inadvertent. We are obliged therefore to come to terms with the situation deliberately contrived by the author; we are driven to consider the relation of all these rules of behaviour, these games and courtesies, to *sin*, morals, the saving of souls, to what the author would have held to be eternal and universal values. And that, surely, is precisely why the confession is introduced, and at this point. Gawain in his last perilous extremity was obliged to tear his 'code' in two, and distinguish its components of good manners and good morals. We are now compelled to consider these matters further.

The first implication of the confession is seen thus to be that retention of the girdle was not a *misdeed* or a *sin* on the moral plane in the author's view. For there are only two alternatives: either (*a*) Gawain did not mention the girdle at all, being sufficiently instructed to distinguish between such pastimes and serious matters; or (*b*) if he did mention it, his confessor *lerned hym better*. The former is perhaps the less likely, since Gawain's education in this direction had, we might say, only just begun; whereas we are told that before he went to confession Gawain asked the advice of the priest.[15]

We have in fact reached the point of intersection of two different planes: of a real and permanent, and an unreal and passing world of values: *morals* on the one hand, and on the other a *code of honour*, or a game with rules. The personal code of most people was, and of many still is, like that of Sir Gawain made up of a close blend of the two; and breaches at any point in that personal code have a very similar emotional flavour. Only a crisis, or serious thought without a crisis (which is rare) will serve to disentangle the elements; and the process may be painful, as Gawain discovered.

A 'game with rules' may deal, of course, with trivial matters or with ones more serious in an ascending scale, as, say, from games with pieces of cardboard upwards. The more they deal with or become involved with real affairs and duties, the more moral bearings they will have; the things 'done' or 'not done' will have two sides, the ritual or rules of the game, and the eternal rules; and therefore the more occasions there will be for a *dilemma*, a conflict of rules. And the more seriously you take your games, the severer and more painful the dilemma. Sir Gawain belonged (as he is depicted) by class, tradition, and training to the kind that take their games with great seriousness. His suffering was acute. He was, one might say, selected for that reason – by an author who belonged to the same class and tradition and knew what it felt like from the inside; but who was interested also in problems of conduct, and have given some thought to them.

It might be felt a fair question to interject at this moment: 'Is it not a *fault of art*, a poetic blunder, to allow so serious a matter as a real confession and absolution to intrude at this point? To force into the open, and compel the attention of a reader to this divergence of values (in which he may not be much interested)? Indeed to intrude such matters at all at any point into a fairy-story, to subject such absurdities as exchanging venison for a kiss to a serious examination?'

I am not at this time greatly concerned to answer such a question; for I am at the moment chiefly anxious to assert, to show (I hope), that this is what the author of *Sir Gawain and the Green Knight* has in fact done, and that his operations upon his material will be unintelligible or largely misunderstood if that is not recognized. But if the question were raised I would reply: There is a strength and life about this poem which is almost universally admitted. This is more likely to be *due* to the greater seriousness of the author than to have survived in spite of it. But much depends on what you want, or think that you want. Do you demand that the author should have the objects that you would expect him to have, or the views that you would prefer him to hold? That he should, for instance, be an anthropological antiquarian? Or that he should simply devote himself to telling an exciting fairy-story well, in such a way as to produce literary credibility sufficient for entertainment? And how will he do that, in terms of his own time and thought? Surely, if that simple object was his only object (unlikely enough in the complex and didactic fourteenth century), he would in the process of giving life to old legends inevitably slide into the consideration of contemporary, or permanent, problems of conduct? It is by that consideration that he has vivified his characters, and by that has given new life to old tales – totally different to their former significance (about which he probably knew,

and certainly cared, much less than some men of this day).
It is a case of pouring new wine into old bottles, no doubt,
and there are some inevitable cracks and leaks. But I at any
rate find this question of ethics both more vivid for its curi-
ous and bizarre setting, and in itself more interesting than
all the guesses about more primitive times. But then I think
the fourteenth century superior to barbarism, and theology
and ethics above folklore.

I do not, of course, insist that the author must have had,
as a conscious purpose, any such object as probing into the
relation of real and artificial rules of conduct when he began
to deal with this story. I imagine this poem took some time to
write, was often altered, expanded here and cut down there.
But the moral questions are there, inherent in the tale, and
they will naturally arise and present themselves for attention
in proportion as the tale is realistically handled, and in pro-
portion as the author is a man of thought and intelligence,
something more than a tale-pedlar. In any case it is clear
that before he achieved his final version the author was fully
aware of what he was doing: writing a 'moral' poem, and a
study of knightly virtue and manners under strain; for he put
in two stanzas ('though it may tarry my story', and though
we may not now like it) about the Pentangle, as he sent off
his knight to his trial. And before he puts in the passage
about confession at the end of the major trial, he has already
drawn our attention to the divergence of values, by the clear
distinction expressed in lines 1773–4; lines which place the
moral law higher than the laws of 'courtesy', and explicitly
reject, and make Gawain reject, *adultery* as part of courtesy
possible to a perfect knight. A very contemporary and very
English point of view![16]

But by the open invitation to adultery of lines 49.1237–40,
and that is no doubt one of the reasons why it is placed at the

beginning, we are able to see the hollowness of all the courteous fencing that follows. For Gawain from that moment can have no doubt whatever of the lady's object: *to haf wonnen hym to woʒe* ('to allure him to love-making', 61.1550). He is attacked on two fronts, and has in reality abandoned from the outset 'service', the absolute submission of the 'true servant' to the will and wishes of the lady; though he strives throughout to maintain the verbal shadow of it, the gentleness of polite speech and manners.

> By God, I would be glad, if good to you seemed
> whatever I could say, or in service could offer
> to the pleasure of your excellence – it would be pure delight
>
> (50.1245–7)

> But I am proud of the praise you are pleased to give me,
> and as your servant in earnest my sovereign I hold you
>
> (51.1277–8)

> All your will I would wish to work, as I am able,
> being so beholden in honour, and, so help me the Lord,
> desiring ever the servant of yourself to remain   (61.1546–8)

All such expressions have become mere pretences, reduced to a level hardly above that of the Christmas games, when the *wylnyng* (1546) of the lady has been and is persistently rejected.

Sheer courtly practice in the game of manners and adroitness of speech enabled Gawain to avoid being openly *craþayn*, to eschew 'vileinye' in words, that is expressions that were boorish or brutally outspoken (whether just and true, or not).[17] But even though he may do it with disarming gracefulness, the law of 'service' to the lady's wishes is in fact broken. And the motive of the breach, of all his adroit defence, can from the first only be a moral one, though this is not stated until 71.1773–4. Had there been no other way out Gawain would have had to abandon even his technical courtesy of manners and *lodly refuse* (1772). But he was never 'driven nearer to the line' than to say: 'Nay! lover have I none, and none will have meanwhile' (71.1790–1), which in spite of his 'smooth smile' is plain enough and *a worde þat worst is of alle* (72.1792). But the lady drives him no further, for undoubtedly the author did not wish the gentleness of Gawain to be broken down. He approved gentle manners and absence of 'vileinye' when allied to, founded on, virtue, the distillation of the courtesy in 'courtly love' without adultery.[18]

We must then recognize that the intrusion of Sir Gawain's confession and its precise placing in the poem was deliberate; and that it is an indication of the author's opinion that *games* and *manners* were not important, ultimately (for 'salvation', 75.1879), and were in any case on an inferior plane to real *virtue*, to which they must in the case of conflict give way. Even the Green Knight recognizes the distinction, and declares that Gawain is 'the most faultless man on earth' (95.2363) with regard to the major moral issue.

But we have not done with the interesting minor issues. The Green Knight proceeds: *Bot here yow lakked a lyttel, sir, and lewté yow wonted* (95.2366). What was this *lewté*? The word is not well translated by 'loyalty', in spite of the kinship of the words; for 'loyalty' is now chiefly applied to honesty and steadfastness in some important personal or public relationship or duty (as to king or country, kin or dear friends). 'Legality' would be equally akin and better; for *lewté* might mean no more than 'sticking to the rules' of whatever grade or sanction. Thus our author can call the alliterations that occur in the proper places in a line, according to merely metrical rules, *lel lettres* 'loyal letters' (2.35).

What rules then is Gawain accused of breaking in accepting, keeping, and concealing the girdle? It might be *three*: accepting a gift without returning one; not surrendering it as part of the 'gain' on the third day (according to a jocular pact, definitely called a *layke* or game); using it as a protection at the tryst. It is plain, I think, that the Green Knight is considering only the *second* of these. He says:

> The true shall truly repay,
> for no peril then need he quake.
> Thou didst fail on the third day ...   (94.2354–6)

> For it is my weed that thou wearest ...   (95.2358)

It is as man to man, as opponents in a game, that he is challenging Gawain. And I think that it is plain that in this he expresses the opinion of the author.

For the author was not a simple-minded man. Those who take an ultimately stern and uncompromising moral view are not necessarily simple-minded. He might think the major issue clear in theory, but nothing in his handling of his tale suggests that he thought moral conduct a simple and painless thing in practice. And anyway he was, as we might say, a gentleman and a sportsman, and was intrigued by the minor issue. Indeed the *moralitas* of his poem, if complicated, is yet also enriched by this exhibition of a clash of rules on a lower plane. He has contrived or brought out a very pretty problem.

Gawain is induced to accept a parting gift from the lady. From the technical fault of 'covetousness' (taking without return) he has been explicitly acquitted: he had nothing he could give in return which would not by its disparity in value be insulting (72. 1798 ff.); he had no thought of the beauty or monetary value of the girdle (81.2037–40). But he was led into a position from which he could not withdraw by the thought that it might possibly save his life when he came to the tryst. Now the author nowhere examines the ethics of the Beheading Game; but if we do so, we shall not find that Gawain had broken any article of his covenant in wearing the girdle for that purpose. All he had promised to do was to come in person, not send a substitute (the probable meaning of line 17.384: *wyth no wyȝ ellez on lyue*, 'in the world with none else but me'); to come at an appointed time, and then stand one stroke without resistance. He does not, therefore, on this count need an advocate; though one might quickly point out that Gawain was actually tricked into the covenant, before the Green Knight revealed that he was magically protected; and his promise might well be held ethically void, and even on the level of a mere 'game' a little private magic of his own could only be regarded as perfectly fair. But the author was not considering this case; though he was not unaware of the point, as we see in Gawain's protest:

> But if on floor now falls my head,
> I cannot it restore.   (91.2282–3)

We are thus merely considering the events in the castle, and the sporting pact with the lord. Gawain had accepted the girdle as a gift because of his dread of the beheading. But again he had been caught. The lady's timing was cunning. She pressed the belt on him, and the moment he weakened she gave it to him, and then closed the trap. She begged him not to tell her husband. He agreed. He could hardly do anything else; but with his characteristic generosity, indeed impetuous excess, which we have already noted, he vowed never to tell anyone else in the world.[19] Of course he desired the belt on the chance (he seems never to have rated it higher than that) that it might save him from death; but even if he had not, he would have been in a dilemma of 'courtesy'. To have rejected the belt, once accepted; or to have refused the request: neither would have been 'courteous'. It was not for him to enquire why he must keep the belt secret; presumably it was to save the lady from embarrassment, since there was no reason to suppose that it was not hers to give. At any rate it was quite as much hers to give as her kisses, and in that matter he had protected her already from embarrassment by refusing to say from whom he had obtained them.[20] It is not said at this moment of acceptance and promise that Gawain recalled his game-compact with the lord at all. But he cannot be finally excused on that ground. For he could not long remain forgetful of the point. When the lord came home at night, he was bound to remember. And he did. It is not said so; but we see it clearly in stanza 77: in Gawain's haste to get the business over. 'This time I will pay first' he cries (as usual going further than he need, whether in making or breaking a promise), as he goes to meet the lord half way (lines 1932–4).

It is at this point then, and at this point only, that we may detect Gawain in a fault, such as it is. 'I shall first fulfil the compact that we made,' he says, and for what that compact was worth he does not do so. He says nothing about the girdle. And he is uneasy. 'Enough!' he cries, when the lord (with a significance that he cannot yet perceive, nor we until we have read the whole tale) says that a fox-fell is poor pay for three such precious things as these kisses.

Well, there it is. *Þrid tyme þrowe best,* but *at þe þrid þou fayled þore.* It is not my part to argue that Gawain did not 'fail' at all; for neither was that the thesis of the author. But to consider in what degree and on what plane he failed, in the author's view, so far as it can be discerned; for with such points he was deeply concerned. There were for him, it seems clear to me from his handling of this tale, *three* planes: mere jesting pastimes, such as that played between Gawain and the lord of the castle; 'courtesy',[21] as a code of 'gentle' or polite manners, which included a special mode of deference to women, and could be held to include, as it was by the lady, the more serious, and therefore more dangerous, 'game' of courtly love-making, which might compete with moral laws; and finally real morals, virtues and sins. These might compete one with another. If so, the higher law must be obeyed. From the first arrival of Sir Gawain at the castle situations are being prepared in which such competitions, with dilemmas in conduct, will occur. The author is chiefly interested in the competition between 'courtesy' and virtue (purity and loyalty); he shows us their increasing divergence, and shows us Gawain at the crisis of the temptation recognizing this, and choosing virtue rather than courtesy, yet preserving a graciousness of manner and a gentleness of speech belonging to the true spirit of courtesy. I think it was his intention by the confession also to show that the lowest grade, 'jesting pastime', was not an ultimately important matter at all; but only after he had amused himself, as it were, by exhibiting a dilemma which artificial courtesy could produce even on a lower level. In this case, since questions of sin and virtue did not arise, Gawain placed the rules of courtesy higher, and obeyed the lady, even though it landed him in breaking his word (though that only in a game of no seriousness). But alas! as I think our author would have said, the rules of artificial courtesy could not really excuse him, not being of universal overriding validity, as are those of morality, not even if courtesy alone had been his motive for taking the girdle. But it was not. He would never have been in the position where he was bound to secrecy, contrary to the games-pact, if he had not wanted to possess the girdle for its possible power: he wished to save his life, a simple and honest motive, and by means that were in no way contrary to his original pact with the Green Knight, and conflicted only with the seemingly absurd and purely jocular pact with the lord of the castle. That was his only fault.

We may observe that each of these 'planes' has its own court of judgement. The moral law is referred to the Church. *Lewté*, 'playing the game' when it is a mere game, as man to man, is referred to the Green Knight, who indeed speaks of the procedure in mock-religious terms, though (it may be noted) he applies these only to the game: the higher matters have been already judged; 'confession' and a 'penance' at the point of his edge. Courtesy is referred to the supreme court of such affairs, the Court of King Arthur of *kydde cortaysye*; and the case against the defendant is laughed out.

But there is yet another court: Sir Gawain himself, and his own judgement. Let us say at once that he is not competent to judge this case impartially, and his judgement cannot be held valid. He is not unnaturally at first in an emotional state of mind, greatly disturbed, after having not only his whole 'code' pulled to pieces, but receiving sore wounds to his pride. His first outcry against himself is hardly more likely to be just than his bitter generalization against women.[22] But it is none the less very interesting to consider what he has to say; because he is a very roundly drawn character, and not a mere vehicle of opinions and analyses. This poet had skill in character drawing. Though the lady, when she has a reported speaking part, has only a simple role, and only one line to follow (directed by an unexplained 'enmity'), all that she says has an unmistakable tone of her own. Better still is Sir Bertilak, and greater the skill with which he is made to behave and speak credibly both as Green Knight and as Host, so that, if these two had not in fact been one, either would have been adequately drawn as an individual, yet at the end we are well able to believe that we have listened to the same character throughout: it is this as much as anything that makes a reader accept as unquestioningly as Gawain their identity without (in this poem) any disenchantment or change of shape after the revelation. But both these actors are secondary, and their main function is to provide the situation for Gawain's trial. Gawain has full literary reality.

His 'perfection' is made more human and credible, and therefore more appreciable as genuine nobility, by the small flaw.[23] But, to my mind, nothing makes him 'come alive' as a real man so much as the depiction of his 'reactions' to the revelation: here that grossly abused word 'reaction' can with some justice be used, for his words and behaviour are largely a matter of instinct and emotion. We may well consider the contrast between the stanzas in which these are exhibited and the lines in which his perilous journeys are described, lines at once picturesque and perfunctory. But this poet was not really interested in fairy-tale or in romance for their own sakes. It is also, I think, a final stroke of art in a poem that is so concentrated on virtue and problems of conduct that it should end with a glimpse of the 'reactions' of a man truly 'gentle', but not deeply reflective, to a fault in a part of his personal code that is not to a cool outside judge essential. That it should indeed end with a glimpse of that twofold scale with which all reasonably charitable people measure: the stricter for oneself, the more lenient for others.[24] *Þe kyng comfortez þe knyt, and alle þe court als laȝen loude þerat.*

What does Gawain feel and say? He accuses himself of *couardise* and *couetyse*. He 'stood in a study' a long while.

in such grief and disgust he had a grue in his heart;
all the blood from his breast in his blush mingled,
and he shrank into himself with shame at that speech.
The first words on that field that he found then to say
were: 'Cursed be ye, Coveting, and Cowardice also!
In you is vileness, and vice that virtue destroyeth.'
He took then the treacherous thing, and untying the knot
fiercely flung he the belt at the feet of the knight:
'See there the falsifier, and foul be its fate!
Through care for thy blow Cowardice brought me
to consent to Coveting, my true kind[25] to forsake,
which is free-hand and faithful word that are fitting to
                                                        knights.
Now I am faulty and false, who afraid have been ever
of treachery and troth-breach: the two now my curse
            may bear!   (95.2370–84)

Later, on return to the Court, he recounts his adventures
in this order:[26] his hardships; the way things went at the tryst,
and the bearing of the Green Knight; the love-making of
the lady; and (last of all) the matter of the Girdle. He then
showed the scar in his neck which he got as a rebuke for his
vnleuté:

> It was torment to tell the truth:
> in his face the blood did flame;
> he groaned for grief and ruth
> when he showed it, to his shame.

'Lo! Lord,' he said at last, and the lace handled,
'This is the band! For this a rebuke I bear in my neck!
This is the grief and disgrace I have got for myself
from the covetousness and cowardice that o'ercame me
                                                        there!

This is the token of the troth-breach that I am detected in,
and needs must I wear it while in the world I remain.'

(100–1.2501–10)

Two lines follow, of which the first is unclear, but which
together (however interpreted or emended) undoubtedly
express Gawain's feeling that nothing can ever delete this
blot. That is in keeping with his 'excess' when moved; but it
is true to the emotions of many others. For one may believe
in the forgiveness of sins (as he did), even forgive oneself
one's own and certainly forget them, but the sting of shame
on morally less important or insignificant levels will bite still
after long years as sharp as new!

Sir Gawain's emotion is thus one of burning shame; and
the burden of his self-accusation is cowardice and covet-
ousness. Cowardice is the chief, for through it he fell into
covetousness. This must mean that as a knight of the Round
Table Gawain makes no claim against the Green Knight for
the unfairness of the beheading-pact (though he has glanced
at it in lines 2282–3), abides by his own words *quat-so bifallez
after* (382), and elects to stand trial on the simple ground
that this was a test of the absolute courage of a knight of his
Order: having given his word he was obliged to keep it even
with death as the consequence, and to meet that with straight
unflinching human courage. He was by circumstance the
representative of the Round Table and should have stood his
ground just so, without aids.

On that simple, but very high level, he is ashamed, and as
a result emotionally disturbed. He thus calls 'cowardice' his
reluctance to throw away his life without striking a blow, or
to surrender a talisman that might possibly have saved him.
He calls 'covetice' his acceptance of a gift from a lady which
he could not immediately repay, though it was pressed on

143

him after two refusals, and in spite of the fact that he did not value it for its costliness. It was indeed only 'covetice' within the terms of the game with the lord of the castle: keeping back any part of the *waith* because he wanted it for himself (for any reason). He calls 'treachery'[27] a breach of the rules of a mere pastime, which he could only have regarded as jocular or whimsical (whatever lay hidden in the proposer of the game), since there could obviously be no real exchange between the gains of a hunter and those of a man idling at home!

And so we end. Beyond that our author does not take us. We have seen a gentle courtly knight learn by bitter experience the perils of Courtesy, and the unreality in the last resort of protestations of complete 'service' to a lady as a 'sovereign' whose will is law;[28] and in that last resort we have seen him prefer a higher law. But though by that higher law he proved 'faultless', the exposure of 'courtesy' of this kind went further, and he has had to suffer the final mortification of discovering that the will of the lady was in fact his own disgrace, and that all her flattering protestations of love were false. In a moment of bitterness he has rejected all his 'cortaysye' and cried against women as deceivers:

> a gain 'twould be vast
> to love them well and believe them not, if it lay in man's
> > power!
> > (97.2420–1)

But that has not been all his suffering as a knight: he has been tricked into 'not playing the game' and breaking his word in a sport; and we have seen him pass through an agony of emotional shame at this failure on a lower plane only really fitting to failure on the higher. This all seems to me vividly true and credible, and I am not making fun of it, if I say that as a final spectacle we see Gawain tearing off the School Tie (as unworthy to wear it), and riding home with a white feather stuck in his cap, only to have that adopted as the colours of the First Eleven, while the matter ends with the laughter of the Court of Honour.

But finally, how true it is to the depicted character of Gawain, this excess of shame, this going beyond all that is required in adopting a badge of disgrace for all to see always, *in tokenyng he watz tane in tech of a faute* (100.2488)! And how true also to the whole tone and air of this poem, so concerned with 'confession' and penance.

> Grace innogh þe mon may haue
> Þat synnez þenne new, ȝif him repente,
> Bot wyth sorȝ and syt he mot it craue,
> And byde þe payne þerto is bent

says the poet in his *Pearl* (661–4).[29] After the shame the repentance, and then the unreserved confession with sorrow and penance, and at last not only forgiveness, but the redemption, so that the 'harm' that is not concealed, and the reproach that is voluntarily borne, becomes a glory, *euermore after*. And with that the whole scene, for a time so vivid, so present, even topical, begins to fade back into the Past. *Gawayn with his olde curteisye* goes back into *Fairye*[30]

> as it is written in the best of the books of romance.
> Thus in Arthur his days happened this marvel,
> as the Book of the Brut beareth us witness;
> since Brutus the bold knight to Britain came first,
> after the siege and the assault had ceased at Troy,
> > I trow,
> > many a marvel such before

has happened here ere now.
To his bliss us bring Who bore
the Crown of Thorns on brow!
Amen.   (101.2521–30)

Postscript: lines 1885–92.*

In the above discussion it was said (page 130) that Gawain's
light heart was sufficient evidence that he had made a 'good
confession'. By that I meant that gaiety proceeding from a
'lightness of heart' may be and often is a result of the fitting
reception of a sacrament by one of the faithful, and that quite
independently of other pains or cares: such as, in Gawain's
case, fear of the blow, fear of death. But this may be, and has
been, queried. It has been asked: Is not his gaiety due rather
to having the belt, and so being no longer afraid of the tryst?
Or it has been suggested that Gawain's mood is due rather to
despair: let me eat and be merry, for tomorrow I die!

We are not dealing with a simple-minded author, nor with
a simple-minded period, and it is not necessary to assume
that only one explanation of Gawain's mood is possible (i.e.
was in the poet's mind). Gawain is being drawn with under-
standing, and he is made to feel, speak, and behave as such
a man would in his situation as a whole: consolation of reli-
gion, magic belt (or at least a belief that such a thing was
possible), and approaching mortal peril, and all. But I think,
nonetheless, that the placing of the lines describing his mood
immediately after the absolution (*And sypen* 1885), and the
use of the words *ioye* and *blys*, are sufficient to show that
the author intended the confession to be the chief reason of
Gawain's increased mirth; and was not thinking at all of a
wild gaiety of despair.

---

* Cited above in translation, p. 130.

But the belt requires more attention. I think it is signifi-
cant that Gawain nowhere ever shows confidence in the gir-
dle's efficacy, certainly not even *hope* in it sufficient to cause
care-free joy! In fact his hope in it seems to have continually
decreased from the time of his confession. It is true that,
at the time of acceptance and before his visit to the priest,
he thanked the lady abundantly and heartily for it (one so
courteous could hardly do less!), but even at the moment
when the idea of help in escaping from death first wakes
in his mind (lines 1855 ff.) and is strongest, before he has
had time to reflect, all that the poet strictly reports him as
thinking is: 'It would be a marvellous thing to have in the
desperate business allotted to me. If I could somehow escape
being slain, it would be a splendid trick.' It does not sound
confident enough, as an explanation of his being merrier
that day than ever before. In any case that night he sleeps
very badly, and hears every cock crow, dreading the hour of
the tryst. In lines 83.2075–6 we read of *þat tene place þer þe
ruful race he schulde resayue* ('that grievous place where he is
due to endure the dolorous blow'), which is plainly meant
to be Gawain's reflexion as he and his guide set out. In lines
85.2138–9 he openly declares to his guide that his trust is
in God, whose servant he is.[31] Similarly in lines 86.2158–9,
with reference certainly to his confession and preparedness
for death, he says: *to Goddez wylle I am ful bayn, and to hym
I haf me tone.* Again in lines 88.2208–11 he overcomes fear
not by any thought or mention of the 'jewel for the jeopardy'
but by submission to God's will. In lines 90.2255 ff. he is in
great fear of imminent death, and is at pains to conceal it,
but does not quite succeed. In lines 91.2265–7 he expected
the stroke to kill him. And finally in lines 92.2307–8 we read:
no meruayle þaȝ hym myslyke þat hoped of no rescowe.

Now all this fear, and this summoning up of courage to

meet death, is perfectly consonant with the consolation of religion and with a mood of joy after being assoiled, but it does not accord at all with possession of a talisman that is *believed in* as a protection against bodily harm, according to the words of the temptress:

> For whoever goes girdled with this green riband,
> while he keeps it well clasped closely about him,
> there is none so hardy under heaven that to hew him were
> > able;
> for he could not be killed by any cunning of hand.
> (74.1851–4)

We may fairly say, then, that from the moment of its acceptance, certainly from the moment of his absolution, the Girdle seems to have been of no comfort to Gawain.[32] If it were not for lines 81.2030–40, where Gawain puts on the Girdle *for gode of hymseluen*, we might well have supposed that he had, after confession, resolved not to use it, though he could not now in courtesy hand it back or break his promise of secrecy. From Gawain's setting out to his shame at the revelation the poet has at any rate ignored the Girdle, or has represented Gawain as doing so. Such comfort and strength as he has beyond his own natural courage is derived only from *religion*. It is no doubt possible to dislike this moral and religious outlook, but the poet has it; and if one does not (with or without dislike) recognize this, the purport and point of the poem will be missed, the point at any rate that the author intended.

Nonetheless it may be objected that I am here pressing the author too hard. If Gawain had shown *no* fear, but had been cheerfully confident in his magic belt (*no more mate ne dismayd for hys mayn dintez* than the Green Knight confident in the magic of Morgan le Fay), then the last scene, the tryst, would have lost all savour. Also granted magic, and even a general belief in the possibility of enchanted belts and the like, it would have needed a very lively faith in this particular belt to take a man to such a tryst without even a shudder of the shoulders! Well, let us concede that. In fact it only goes to strengthen the point that I put forward. Gawain is *not* depicted as having a very lively faith in the Girdle, even if that is only, or partly, for mere reasons of narrative. Therefore his 'joy' on New Year's Eve is not derived from it. Therefore that must be derived from the absolution, to which it is appended, and Gawain is shown as a man with a 'good conscience' and the confession was not 'sacrilegious'.

But quite apart from narrative technique, the poet evidently intended to emphasize the moral and (if you will) higher sides of Gawain's character. For that is simply what he has consistently done throughout, whether with complete appropriateness to his inherited story-material or not. And so, while Gawain does not accept the Girdle solely out of courtesy, and is tempted by the hope of magic aid, and when arming does not forget it, but puts it on *for gode of hymseluen* and *to sauen hymself*, this motive is minimized, and Gawain is not represented as relying on it at all when coming to the desperate point – for it, no less than the horrible Green Knight, and his *faierie*, and all *faierie*, is ultimately under God. A reflexion which makes the magic Girdle seem rather feeble, as no doubt the poet intended that it should.

We are meant then to look on Sir Gawain, after his last confession, as clear in conscience, and so able as much as any other brave and pious man (if not as much as a saint) to support himself in the expectation of death with the thought of God's ultimate protection of the righteous. This implies not only that he has survived the lady's temptations, but that his whole adventure and tryst are *for him* righteous, or at least justified and lawful. We now see the great importance of the description in the First Fit of the way in which Sir Gawain became involved in the affair, and the purpose of the remarkable criticisms of King Arthur voiced in the court (in the Second Fit, stanza 29). In these ways Gawain is shown to have become imperilled not out of *nobelay*, nor because of any fantastic custom or vainglorious vow, nor because of pride in prowess or rating himself as the best knight of his Order – all the possible motives that from a strictly moral point of view might make the whole affair for him foolish or reprehensible, a mere wilful risk or waste of life for no sufficient cause. The wilfulness and the pride are cast on the King; Gawain is involved out of humility, and as a matter of duty to his king and kinsman.

We can imagine indeed the author inserting this curious passage after reflexion. After making Gawain's conduct in his adventure the subject of moral analysis on a serious plane, he would see that in that case the adventure must be for Gawain praiseworthy, as judged on the same level. In fact the author has taken this story, or blend of stories, with all its improbabilities, its lack of secure rational motives, and its incoherence, and endeavoured to make it the *machinery* by which a virtuous man is involved in a mortal peril which it is noble, or at least proper (not wrong or silly), for him to face; and is thus drawn into consequent temptations which he does not wilfully or wittingly incur. And in the end he survives all with plain moral weapons. The Pentangle is thus seen to replace the Gryphon on Gawain's shield as part of a deliberate plan throughout – throughout the final version which we have, at any rate. That plan, and that choice and emphasis, must be recognized.

It is another question whether this treatment is either

justified, or artistically successful. For myself, I would say that the criticism of Arthur, and the making of Gawain a proxy of the king with wholly humble and unselfish motives, is for this poem[33] necessary, and successful, and realistic. The Pentangle is justified, and only unsuccessful (at least to my taste, and to that I suppose of many of my period) because it is 'pedantic', very fourteenth-century, almost Chaucerian, in its pedantry indeed, and over long and elaborate, and (most of all) because it proved too difficult for the author's skill with the alliterative verse that he uses. The treatment of the Girdle, hesitating between belief and disregard, is reasonably successful, if one does not scrutinize this matter too closely. A degree of belief in it is necessary for the last temptation-scene; and it proves the only effective bait that the lady has for her traps, thus leading to the one 'flaw' (on the lowest plane of 'playing the game') which makes the actual conduct of Gawain and his near-perfection so much more credible than the mathematical perfection of the Pentangle.

But this belief, or hope, must be played down at the beginning of the last Fit, even if it were in a mere romance unconcerned with moral issues, for confidence in the Girdle would even in such a tale spoil the last scenes. The weakness of the Girdle, as a talisman able (or believed able) to defend a man from wounds, is inherent. Actually this weakness is *less* glaring than it might be, precisely because of the seriousness of the author and the piety which he has ascribed to his pattern of knights; for the disregard of the talisman at the crisis is more credible in such a character as the Gawain of this poem than in a mere adventurer. And yet I regret, not the flaw in Gawain, not that the lady found one little bait for her victim, but that the poet could not think of anything else which Gawain might have accepted and been induced to conceal, and yet one which would not have affected his view of his perilous tryst. But I cannot think of one; so that such criticism, *kesting such cavillacioun*, is idle.

Sir Gawain and the Green Knight remains the best conceived and shaped narrative poem of the Fourteenth Century, indeed of the Middle Age, in English, with one exception only. It has a rival, a claimant to equality not superiority, in Chaucer's masterpiece *Troilus and Criseyde*. That is larger, longer, more intricate, and perhaps more subtle, though no wiser or more perceptive, and certainly less noble. And both these poems deal, from different angles, with the problems that so much occupied the English mind: the relations of Courtesy and Love with morality and Christian morals and the Eternal Law.

1   Of this name *pentangle* he is the first recorded user in the vernacular, the only user indeed in Middle English. Yet he claims that the English call it everywhere the Endless Knot. This much at least may be said: the lack of record must be accidental, for the form that he uses, *penta(u)ngel,* is one that shows already clear traces of popular use, being altered from the correct learned *pentaculum* by association with 'angle'. Moreover, though much concerned with the symbolism, he speaks as if his audience could visualize the shape of the figure.

2   The attempt to describe the complex figure and its symbolism was actually too much even for our poet's considerable skill with the long alliterative line. In any case, since part of its significance was the *interrelation* of religious faith, piety, and courtesy in human relations, the attempt to enumerate 'virtues' brings out the arbitrariness of their division and their individual names at any one time, and the constant flux of the meaning of these names (such as *pité* or *fraunchyse*) from age to age.

3   And why the pentangle is proper to that prince so noble
       I intend now to tell you, though it may tarry my story.

                                  (27.623–4)

4   Though actually it has, I think, tended to be over-elaborated in criticism. One point only has been neglected, as far as my knowledge goes: the author has taken care to show that the lord himself in person, not the hunt generally, slew and obtained the *waith* that he surrendered to Gawain. This is of course clear in the cases of the boar and the fox. But even in the first hunt it is indicated: 'When the sun began to slope he had slain such a number / of does and other deer one might doubt it were true' (53.1321–2). But (since there appear to have been no other persons of rank at the hunt) the lord of the castle is probably the *best* of 1325, who

supervises the cutting up of his own selected 'quarry'. In this case *didden* of 1327 is one of the many errors of the MS, with plural substituted for singular according to the immediate suggestion of a context not wholly clear to the copyist. It was the lord who chose the fattest of his own 'kill' and gave orders for their proper dressing ready for the presentation of *his venysoun* (1375). This may seem a minute point, and remote from the things that are here being considered, but it is, I believe, related to the topic of *lewté* and keeping one's word which is to be examined.

5 Unless perhaps in the minds of those with too much literary experience. Yet evenxc they must realise that we are supposed to see things with Gawain's eyes, and sense the air with his senses, and he has plainly no suspicions.

6 I mean, if we had posed the author with this question, he would have had an answer, for he had thought the whole thing out, especially all that had a moral aspect; and I think that his answer would have been, in the idiom of his time, the one that I am trying to give.

7 His resistance thus actually redounds all the more to his credit, for he is unaware of any peril save that of 'sin', and he resists on plain moral grounds, unaided by the fear of magic powers or even of discovery.

8 The text as typed had: 'could not attain. Or would not. For this [is] a mode of making felt the real tension that one should feel in a narrative of moral struggle.' When 'could not attain' was changed to 'could hardly attain' the following sentence was bracketed as if for exclusion. [Ed.]

9 This statement is the author's. On this matter see the Preface. [Ed.]

10 Written in pencil on the typescript: 'a sacrifice he is not yet prepared to make' – to be placed either at the end of the sentence or after 'without breaking his word'. [Ed.]

11 A cad and a boor.

12 The reference is to *Sir Gawain and the Green Knight* edited by Sir Israel Gollancz, Early English Text Society 1940, p. 123, note to line 1880. [Ed.]

13 And one, it may be added, who beyond any real doubt also wrote *Pearl,* not to mention *Purity* and *Patience.*

14 Since the effectiveness of confession is wholly dependent on the

dispositions of the penitent, and no words of the priest can remedy bad intentions, or the wilful concealment of recollected sin.

15 I do not assert, of course, that a *genuine compact,* even in sport, has never any moral implications, and never involves any obligations. But I do mean that in the author's view 'Christmas games' such as those played by the lord and Gawain are not of that order. To that point I will return.

16 That Gawain appends to *synne* a consideration that makes the sin more heinous or odious, the treachery of a guest to his host, is both ethically sound, and true to character. It is also very proper to this poem which is concerned with *loyalty* on every plane. Here we find Gawain rejecting a *disloyalty* that would really have been sinful, so that we may view the *lack of loyalty* of which he is after accused in its proper scale.

17 So Chaucer reports of his *perfit gentil knight* that *he neuer yet no vileinye ne sayde … unto no maner wight;* and later defends himself speciously against a charge of *vileinye* (precisely low and coarse speech) that might be levelled against his ignoble tales and characters.

18 Whether he would have called the lady's invitation *vileinye* is another matter. The actions of the lord and lady are not in fact judged at all. It is only Gawain's conduct, as the representative of Courtesy and Piety, that is scrutinized. The deeds and words of others are in the main used solely to provide the situations in which his character and behaviour will be exhibited.

19 Which he later expiates, in the same spirit, by telling everyone.

20 Though we might feel, if we were disposed to subject this fairy-tale detail to a scrutiny it is hardly substantial enough to bear, that a kiss cannot be paid away, and at any rate if its source is not named, then a wife's kiss cannot rightly be said to have been surrendered to the husband. But even this point has not been unnoted by the author. The two feinted blows may have been *boute scape* (94.2353), as far as Gawain's flesh went, but they were painful to endure. The Green Knight (or Sir Bertilak) does not seem to have felt that taking kisses from his wife was a matter entirely negligible, even if 'courtesy' was the reason for their acceptance.

21 In the ordinary mundane senses. If our author also wrote the *Pearl* (as seems to me certain), he has complicated matters, for those

who wish to consider his mind and views as a whole, by there using 'courtesy' in a more elevated sense: the manners not of earthly courts, but of the Court of Heaven; the Divine Generosity and Grace, and the unalloyed humility and charity of the Blessed; the spirit, that is, from which even mundane 'courtesy' must proceed, if it is to be alive and sincere, and also pure. There is probably a trace of this to be seen in the conjunction of *clannes* and *cortaysye* (28.653) in the 'fifth five' of the Pentangle which is concerned with virtue in human relationships.

22 This may appear at first to be a blemish, even if the only serious blemish in this poem. It is indeed, I think, put into a form hardly suitable to Gawain, so that it reads rather more like a sentence of *auctor,* a piece of clerkly pedantry. But fundamentally it is in character, true to the general character of Gawain as depicted, and credible to his 'reaction' at the particular moment. Gawain always tends to go a little further than the case requires. He only needs to say: many greater men than I have been deceived by women, so there is some excuse for me. He need not proceed to say that it would be vastly to men's profit if they could love women and yet never trust them at all. But he does. And that is not only very like this Gawain, but not unnatural in any 'courtier' whose very courtesy and pride in it has been made the means of exposing him to shame. Let it be a mere game and pretence, then! he cries – at that moment.

23 Though one may reflect that his near-perfection would not have been attained unless he had set before himself as an ideal the absolute or mathematical perfection symbolized by the Pentangle.

24 The more charitable, the wider often the divergence, as may be seen in the self-stern saints.

25 By the word *kynde* in the original the author may intend Gawain's natural character; but the less introspective sense 'my sort', the proper behaviour of members of his order (knights), is perhaps better.

26 The order is probably not significant (nor strictly possible), except the reservation of the Girdle to the last.

27 Not always so strong a word as now, however, when the association with 'treason' and 'traitor' (originally unconnected) has made it applicable only to acts of great baseness and serious injury.

28 Unless she herself obeys some higher law than herself or than 'love'.

29 In my father's translation of *Pearl* these lines are rendered:
> Grace enow may the man receive
> Who sins anew, if he repent;
> But craving it he must sigh and grieve
> And abide what pains are consequent. [Ed.]

30 Chaucer, *The Squire's Tale,* lines 95–6. The passage in which these lines occur was (in part) the basis for my father's view, mentioned at the beginning of this lecture (p. 111), that Chaucer knew *Sir Gawain and the Green Knight.* [Ed.]

31 Though God's instrument could indeed be the Girdle, in a world where such things were possible, and lawful.

32 It is an interesting point, which cannot have been unintended on the part of the poet, that the belt for which Gawain broke the rules of his game, and so made the only flaw in the perfection of his conduct on all levels, was never in fact of any use to him at all, not even as a hope.

33 It might be regarded as regrettable in Arthurian Romance as a whole. Personally I do not think that belittling of the King (as *sumquat childgered,* and the like) does that any good at all.

Pearl

When *Pearl* was first read in modern times it was accepted as what it purports to be, an elegy on the death of a child, the poet's daughter. The personal interpretation was first questioned in 1904 by W. H. Schofield, who argued that the maiden of the poem was an allegorical figure of a kind usual in medieval vision literature, an abstraction representing 'clean maidenhood'. His view was not generally accepted, but it proved the starting-point of a long debate between the defenders of the older view and the exponents of other theories: that the whole poem is an allegory, though each interpreter has given it a different meaning; or that it is no more than a theological treatise in verse. Much space would be required to rehearse this debate, even in brief summary, and the labour would be unprofitable; but it has not been entirely wasted, for much learning has gone into it, and study has deepened the appreciation of the poem and brought out more clearly the allegorical and symbolical elements that it certainly includes.

A clear distinction between 'allegory' and 'symbolism' may be difficult to maintain, but it is proper, or at least useful, to limit allegory to narrative, to an account (however short) of events; and symbolism to the use of visible signs or things to represent other things or ideas. Pearls were a symbol of purity that especially appealed to the imagination of the Middle Ages (and notably of the fourteenth century);

but this does not make a person who wears pearls, or even one who is called Pearl, or Margaret, into an allegorical figure. To be an 'allegory' a poem must *as a whole*, and with fair consistency, describe in other terms some event or process; its entire narrative and all its significant details should cohere and work together to this end. There are minor allegories within *Pearl*; the parable of the workers in the vineyard (stanzas 42–49) is a self-contained allegory; and the opening stanzas of the poem, where the pearl slips from the poet's hand through the grass to the ground, is an allegory in little of the child's death and burial. But an allegorical description of an event does not make that event itself allegorical. And this initial use is only one of the many applications of the pearl symbol, intelligible if the reference of the poem is personal, incoherent if one seeks for total allegory. For there are a number of precise details in *Pearl* that cannot be subordinated to any general allegorical interpretation, and these details are of special importance since they relate to the central figure, the maiden of the vision, in whom, if anywhere, the allegory should be concentrated and without disturbance.

The basis of criticism, then, must be the references to the child or maiden, and to her relations with the dreamer; and no good reason has ever been found for regarding these as anything but statements of 'fact': the real experiences that lie at the foundation of the poem.

When the dreamer first sees the maiden in the paradisal garden, he says (stanza 21):

> Art þou my perle þat I haf playned,
> Regretted by myn one on nyȝte?
> Much longeyng haf I for þe layned
> Syþen into gresse þou my aglyȝte.

This explains for us the minor allegory of the opening stan-
zas and reveals that the pearl he lost was a maid-child who
died. For the maiden of the vision accepts the identification,
and herself refers to her death in stanza 64. In stanza 35
she says she was at that time very young, and the dreamer
himself in stanza 41 tells us that she was not yet two years
old and had not yet learned her creed or prayers. The whole
theological argument that follows assumes the infancy of the
child when she left this world.

The actual relationship of the child in the world to the
dreamer is referred to in stanza 20: when he first espied her
in his vision he recognized her; he knew her well, he had seen
her before (stanza 14); and so now beholding her visible on
the farther bank of the stream he was the happiest man 'from
here to Greece', for

> Ho watȝ me nerre þen aunte or nece.

'She was more near akin to me than aunt or niece.' *Nerre*
can in the language of the time only mean here 'nearer in
blood relationship'. In this sense it was normal and very fre-
quent. And although it is true that 'nearer than aunt or niece'
might, even so, refer to a sister, the disparity in age makes the
assumption of this relationship far less probable. The depth
of sorrow portrayed for a child so young belongs rather to
parenthood. And there seems to be a special significance in
the situation where the doctrinal lesson given by the celestial
maiden comes from one of no earthly wisdom to her proper
teacher and instructor in the natural order.

A modern reader may be ready to accept the personal
basis of the poem, and yet may feel that there is no need to
assume any immediate or particular foundation in autobiog-
raphy. It is admittedly not necessary for the vision, which is

plainly presented in literary or scriptural terms; the bereavement and the sorrow may also be imaginative fictions, adopted precisely because they heighten the interest of the theological discussion between the maiden and the dreamer.

This raises a difficult and important question for general literary history: whether the purely fictitious 'I' had yet appeared in the fourteenth century, a first person feigned as narrator who had no existence outside the imagination of the real author. Probably not; at least not in the kind of literature that we are here dealing with: visions related by a dreamer. The fictitious traveller had already appeared in 'Sir John Mandeville', the writer of whose 'voyages' seems not to have borne that name, nor indeed, according to modern critics, ever to have journeyed far beyond his study; and it is difficult to decide whether this is a case of fraud intended to deceive (as it certainly did), or an example of prose fiction (in the literary sense) still wearing the guise of truth according to contemporary convention.

This convention was strong, and not so 'conventional' as it may appear to modern readers. Although by those of literary experience it might, of course, be used as nothing more than a device to secure literary credibility (as often by Chaucer), it represented a deep-rooted habit of mind, and was strongly associated with the moral and didactic spirit of the times. Tales of the past required their grave authorities, and tales of new things at least an eyewitness, the author. This was one of the reasons for the popularity of visions: they allowed marvels to be placed within the real world, linking them with a person, a place, a time, while providing them with an explanation in the phantasies of sleep, and a defence against critics in the notorious deception of dreams. So even explicit allegory was usually presented as a thing seen in sleep. How far any such narrated vision, of the more serious kind, was supposed to resemble an actual dream experience is another question. A modern poet would indeed be very unlikely to put forward for factual acceptance a dream that in any way resembled the vision of *Pearl*, even when all allowance is made for the arrangement and formalizing of conscious art. But we are dealing with a period when men, aware of the vagaries of dreams, still thought that amid their japes came visions of truth. And their waking imagination was strongly moved by symbols and the figures of allegory, and filled vividly with the pictures evoked by the scriptures, directly or through the wealth of medieval art. And they thought that on occasion, as God willed, to some that slept blessed faces appeared and prophetic voices spoke. To them it might not seem so incredible that the dream of a poet, one wounded with a great bereavement and troubled in spirit, might resemble the vision in *Pearl*.* However that may be, the narrated vision in the more serious medieval writing represented, if not an actual dream at least a real process of thought culminating in some resolution or turning-point of the interior life – as with Dante, and in *Pearl*. And in all forms, lighter or more grave, the 'I' of the dreamer remained the eyewitness, the author, and facts that he referred to outside the dream (especially those concerning himself) were on a different plane, meant to be taken as literally true, and even by modern critics so taken. In the *Divina Commedia* the *Nel mezzo del cammin di nostra vita* of the opening line, or *la decenne sete* of *Purgatorio xxxii*, are held to refer to real dates and events, the thirty-fifth year of Dante's life in 1300,

---

* Ek oother seyn that thorugh impressiouns,
  As if a wight hath faste a thyng in mynde,
  That thereof comen swiche avysiouns.
  (*Troilus and Criseyde*, v. 372–4)

and the death of Beatrice Portinari in 1290. Similarly the references to Malvern in the Prologue and Passus VII of *Piers Plowman*, and the numerous allusions to London, are taken as facts in someone's life, whoever the critic may favour as the author (or authors) of the poem.

It is true that the 'dreamer' may become a shadowy figure of small biographical substance. There is little left of the actual Chaucer in the 'I' who is the narrator in *The Boke of the Duchesse*. Few will debate how much autobiography there is in the bout of insomnia that is made the occasion of the poem. Yet this fictitious and conventional vision is founded on a real event: the death of Blanche, the wife of John of Gaunt, in 1369. That was her real name, White (as she is called in the poem). However heightened the picture may be that is drawn of her loveliness and goodness, her sudden death was a lamentable event. Certainly it can have touched Chaucer far less deeply than the death of one 'nearer than aunt or niece'; but even so, it is this living drop of reality, this echo of sudden death and loss in the world, that gives to Chaucer's early poem a tone and feeling that raises it above the literary devices out of which he made it. So with the much greater poem *Pearl*, it is overwhelmingly more probable that it too was founded on a real sorrow, and drew its sweetness from a real bitterness.

And yet to the particular criticism of the poem decision on this point is not of the first importance. A feigned elegy remains an elegy; and feigned or unfeigned, it must stand or fall by its art. The reality of the bereavement will not save the poetry if it is bad, nor lend it any interest save to those who are in fact interested, not in poetry, but in documents, whose hunger is for history or biography or even for mere names. It is on general grounds, and considering its period in particular, that a 'real' or directly autobiographical basis for *Pearl* seems likely, since that is the most probable explanation of its form and its poetic quality. And for this argument the discovery of biographical details would have little importance. Of all that has been done in this line the only suggestion of value was made by Sir Israel Gollancz:* that the child may have been actually called a pearl by baptismal name, *Margarita* in Latin, *Margery* in English. It was a common name at the time, because of the love of pearls and their symbolism, and it had already been borne by several saints. If the child was really baptized a pearl, then the many pearls threaded on the strands of the poem in multiple significance receive yet another lustre. It is on such accidents of life that poetry crystallizes:

> And goode faire White she het;
> That was my lady name ryght
> She was bothe fair and bryght;
> She hadde not hir name wrong.
> > (*Boke of the Duchesse*, 948–51).
> 'O perle', quod I, 'in perleʒ pyʒt,
> Art þou my perle þat I haf playned?'

It has been objected that the child as seen in Heaven is not like an infant of two in appearance, speech, or manners: she addresses her father formally as *sir*, and shows no filial affection for him. But this is an apparition of a spirit, a soul not yet reunited with its body after the resurrection, so that theories relevant to the form and age of the glorified and risen body do not concern us. And as an immortal spirit, the

* Edition of *Pearl*, p. xliii: 'He perhaps named the child "Margery" or "Marguerite".' The form Marguerite would not have been used; it is a modern French form.

maiden's relations to the earthly man, the father of her body, are altered. She does not deny his fatherhood, and when she addresses him as *sir* she only uses the form of address that was customary for medieval children. Her part is in fact truly imagined. The sympathy of readers may now go out more readily to the bereaved father than to the daughter, and they may feel that he is treated with some hardness. But it is the hardness of truth. In the manner of the maiden is portrayed the effect upon a clear intelligence of the persistent earthliness of the father's mind; all is revealed to him, and he has eyes, yet he cannot see. The maiden is now filled with the spirit of celestial charity, desiring only his eternal good and the cure of his blindness. It is not her part to soften him with pity, or to indulge in childish joy at their reunion. The final consolation of the father was not to be found in the recovery of a beloved daughter, as if death had not after all occurred or had no significance, but in the knowledge that she was redeemed and saved and had become a queen in Heaven. Only by resignation to the will of God, and through death, could he rejoin her.

And this is the main *purpose* of the poem as distinct from its genesis or literary form: the doctrinal theme, in the form of an argument on salvation, by which the father is at last convinced that his Pearl, as a baptized infant and innocent, is undoubtedly saved, and, even more, admitted to the blessed company of the 144,000 that follow the Lamb. But the doctrinal theme is, in fact, inseparable from the literary form of the poem and its occasion; for it arises directly from the grief, which imparts deep feeling and urgency to the whole discussion. Without the elegiac basis and the sense of great personal loss which pervades it, *Pearl* would indeed be the mere theological treatise on a special point, which some critics have called it. But without the theological debate the grief would never have risen above the ground. Dramatically the debate represents a long process of thought and mental struggle, an experience as real as the first blind grief of bereavement. In his first mood, even if he had been granted a vision of the blessed in Heaven, the dreamer would have received it incredulously or rebelliously. And he would have awakened by the mound again, not in the gentle and serene resignation of the last stanza, but still as he is first seen, looking only backward, his mind filled with the horror of decay, wringing his hands, while his *wreched wylle in wo ay wrazte.*

Pearl

PEARL of delight that a prince doth please
    To grace in gold enclosed so clear,
I vow that from over orient seas
Never proved I any in price her peer.
So round, so radiant ranged by these,
So fine, so smooth did her sides appear
That ever in judging gems that please
Her only alone I deemed as dear.
Alas! I lost her in garden near:
Through grass to the ground from me it shot;
I pine now oppressed by love-wound drear
For that pearl, mine own, without a spot.

2   Since in that spot it sped from me,
I have looked and longed for that precious thing
That me once was wont from woe to free,
to uplift my lot and healing bring,
But my heart doth hurt now cruelly,
My breast with burning torment sting.
Yet in secret hour came soft to me
The sweetest song I e'er heard sing;
Yea, many a thought in mind did spring
To think that her radiance in clay should rot.
O mould! Thou marrest a lovely thing,
My pearl, mine own, without a spot.

3   In that spot must needs be spices spread
Where away such wealth to waste hath run;
Blossoms pale and blue and red
There shimmer shining in the sun;
No flower nor fruit their hue may shed
Where it down into darkling earth was done,
For all grass must grow from grains that are dead,
No wheat would else to barn be won.
From good all good is ever begun,
And fail so fair a seed could not,
So that sprang and sprouted spices none
From that precious pearl without a spot.

4   That spot whereof I speak I found
When I entered in that garden green,
As August's season high came round
When corn is cut with sickles keen.
There, where that pearl rolled down, a mound
With herbs was shadowed fair and sheen,
With gillyflower, ginger, and gromwell crowned,
And peonies powdered all between.
If sweet was all that there was seen,
Fair, too, a fragrance flowed I wot,
Where dwells that dearest, as I ween,
My precious pearl without a spot.

5   By that spot my hands I wrung dismayed;
For care full cold that had me caught
A hopeless grief on my heart was laid.
Though reason to reconcile me sought,
For my pearl there prisoned a plaint I made,
In fierce debate unmoved I fought;

Be comforted Christ Himself me bade,
But in woe my will ever strove distraught.
On the flowery plot I fell, methought;
Such odour through my senses shot,
I slipped and to sudden sleep was brought,
O'er that precious pearl without a spot.

6   FROM that spot my spirit sprang apace,
     On the turf my body abode in trance;
My soul was gone by God's own grace
Adventuring where marvels chance.
I knew not where in the world was that place
Save by cloven cliffs was set my stance;
And towards a forest I turned my face,
Where rocks in splendour met my glance;
From them did a glittering glory lance,
None could believe the light they lent;
Never webs were woven in mortal haunts
Of half such wealth and wonderment.

7   Wondrous was made each mountain-side
With crystal cliffs so clear of hue;
About them woodlands bright lay wide,
As Indian dye their boles were blue;
The leaves did as burnished silver slide
That thick upon twigs there trembling grew.
When glades let light upon them glide
They shone with a shimmer of dazzling hue.
The gravel on ground that I trod with shoe
Was of precious pearls of the Orient:
Sunbeams are blear and dark to view
Compared with that fair wonderment.

8   In wonder at those fells so fair
     My sold all grief forgot let fall;
     Odours so fresh of fruits there were,
     I was fed as by food celestial.
     In the woods the birds did wing and pair,
     Of flaming hues, both great and small;
     But cithern-string and glittern-player
     Their merry mirth could ne'er recall,
     For when they beat their pinions all
     In harmony their voices blent:
     No delight more lovely could men enthrall
     Than behold and hear that wonderment.

9   Thus arrayed was all in wonderment
     That forest where forth my fortune led;
     No man its splendour to present
     With tongue could worthy words have said.
     I walked ever onward well-content;
     No hill was so tall that it stayed my tread;
     More fair the further afield I went
     Were plants, and fruits, and spices spread;
     Through hedge and mead lush waters led
     As in strands of gold there steeply pent.
     A river I reached in cloven bed:
     O Lord! the wealth of its wonderment!

10   The adornments of that wondrous deep
     Were beauteous banks of beryl bright:
     Swirling sweetly its waters sweep,
     Ever rippling on in murmurous flight.
     In the depths stood dazzling stones aheap
     As a glitter through glass that glowed with light,

As streaming stars when on earth men sleep
Stare in the welkin in winter night;
For emerald, sapphire, or jewel bright
Was every pebble in pool there pent,
And the water was lit with rays of light,
Such wealth was in its wonderment.

11 THE wondrous wealth of down and dales,
of wood and water and lordly plain,
My mirth makes mount: my mourning fails,
My care is quelled and cured my pain.
Then down a stream that strongly sails
I blissful turn with teeming brain;
The further I follow those flowing vales
The more strength of joy my heart doth strain.
As fortune fares where she doth deign,
Whether gladness she gives or grieving sore,
So he who may her graces gain,
His hap is to have ever more and more.

12 There more was of such marvels thrice
Than I could tell, though I long delayed;
For earthly heart could not suffice
For a tithe of the joyful joys displayed.
Therefore I thought that Paradise
Across those banks was yonder laid;
I weened that the water by device
As bounds between pleasances was made;
Beyond that stream by steep or slade
That city's walls I weened must soar;
But the water was deep, I dared not wade,
And ever I longed to, more and more.

13 More and more, and yet still more,
   I fain beyond the stream had scanned,
   For fair as was this hither shore,
   Far lovelier was the further land.
   To find a ford I did then explore,
   And round about did stare and stand;
   But perils pressed in sooth more sore
   The further I strode along the strand.
   I should not, I thought, by fear be banned
   From delights so lovely that lay in store;
   But a happening new then came to hand
   That moved my mind ever more and more.

14 A marvel more did my mind amaze:
   I saw beyond that border bright
   From a crystal cliff the lucent rays
   And beams in splendour lift their light.
   A child abode there at its base:
   She wore a gown of glistening white,
   A gentle maid of courtly grace;
   Erewhile I had known her well by sight.
   As shredded gold that glistered bright
   She shone in beauty upon the shore;
   Long did my glance on her alight,
   And the longer I looked I knew her more.

15 The more I that face so fair surveyed,
   When upon her gracious form I gazed,
   Such gladdening glory upon me played
   As my wont was seldom to see upraised.
   Desire to call her then me swayed,
   But dumb surprise my mind amazed;

In place so strange I saw that maid,
The blow might well my wits have crazed.
Her forehead fair then up she raised
That hue of polished ivory wore.
It smote my heart distraught and dazed,
And ever the longer, the more and more.

16 MORE than I would my dread did rise.
    I stood there still and dared not call
With closed mouth and open eyes,
I stood as tame as hawk in hall.
A ghost was present, I did surmise,
And feared for what might then befall,
Lest she should flee before mine eyes
Ere I to tryst could her recall.
So smooth, so seemly, slight and small,
That flawless fair and mirthful maid
Arose in robes majestical,
A precious gem in pearls arrayed.

17 There pearls arrayed and royally dight
Might one have seen by fortune graced
When fresh as flower-de-luces bright
She down to the water swiftly paced
In linen robe of glistening white,
With open sides that seams enlaced
With the merriest margery-pearls my sight
Ever before, I vow, had traced.
Her sleeves hung long below her waist
Adorned with pearls in double braid;
Her kirtle matched her mande chaste
All about with precious pearls arrayed.

18 A crown arrayed too wore that girl
   Of margery-stones and others none,
   With pinnacles of pure white pearl
   That perfect flowers were figured on.
   On head nought else her hair did furl,
   And it framed, as it did round her run.
   Her countenance grave for duke or earl,
   And her hue as rewel ivory wan.
   As shredded sheen of gold then shone
   Her locks on shoulder loosely laid.
   Her colour pure was surpassed by none
   Of the pearls in purfling rare arrayed.

19 Arrayed was wristlet, and the hems were dight
   At hands, at sides, at throat so fair
   With no gem but the pearl all white
   And burnished white her garments were;
   But a wondrous pearl unstained and bright
   She amidst her breast secure did bear;
   Ere mind could fathom its worth and might
   Man's reason thwarted would despair.
   No tongue could in worthy words declare
   The beauty that was there displayed,
   It was so polished, pure, and fair,
   That precious pearl on her arrayed.

20 In pearls arrayed that maiden free
   Beyond the stream came down the strand.
   From here to Greece none as glad could be
   As I on shore to see her stand,
   Than aunt or niece more near to me:
   The more did joy my heart expand.

She deigned to speak, so sweet was she,
Bowed low as ladies' ways demand.
With her crown of countless worth in hand
A gracious welcome she me bade.
My birth I blessed, who on the strand
To my love replied in pearls arrayed.

21 'O Pearl!' said I, 'in pearls arrayed,
Are you my pearl whose loss I mourn?
Lament alone by night I made,
Much longing I have hid for thee forlorn,
Since to the grass you from me strayed.
While I pensive waste by weeping worn,
Your life of joy in the land is laid
Of Paradise by strife untorn.
What fate hath hither my jewel borne
And made me mourning's prisoner?
Since asunder we in twain were torn,
I have been a joyless jeweller.'

22 That jewel in gems so excellent
Lifted her glance with eyes of grey,
Put on her crown of pearl-orient,
And gravely then began to say:
'Good sir, you have your speech mis-spent
To say your pearl is all away
That is in chest so choicely pent,
Even in this gracious garden gay,
Here always to linger and to play
Where regret nor grief e'er trouble her.
"Here is a casket safe" you would say,
If you were a gentle jeweller.

23 But, jeweller gentle, if from you goes
    Your joy through a gem that you held lief,
    Methinks your mind toward madness flows
    And frets for a fleeting cause of grief.
    For what you lost was but a rose
    That by nature failed after flowering brief;
    Now the casket's virtues that it enclose
    Prove it a pearl of price in chief;
    And yet you have called your fate a thief
    That of naught to aught hath fashioned her,
    You grudge the healing of your grief,
    You are no grateful jeweller.'

24 Then a jewel methought had now come near,
    And jewels the courteous speech she made.
    'My blissful one,' quoth I, 'most dear,
    My sorrows deep you have all allayed.
    To pardon me I pray you here!
    In the darkness I deemed my pearl was laid;
    I have found it now, and shall make good cheer,
    With it dwell in shining grove and glade,
    And praise all the laws that my Lord hath made,
    Who hath brought me near such bliss with her.
    Now could I to reach you these waters wade,
    I should be a joyful jeweller.'

25 'Jeweller', rejoined that jewel clean,
    'Why jest ye men? How mad ye be!
    Three things at once you have said, I ween:
    Thoughtless, forsooth, were all the three.
    You know not on earth what one doth mean;
    Your words from your wits escaping flee:

You believe I live here on this green,
Because you can with eyes me see;
Again, you will in this land with me
Here dwell yourself, you now aver;
And thirdly, pass this water free:
That may no joyful jeweller.

26 I hold that jeweller worth little praise
    Who well esteems what he sees with eye,
And much to blame his graceless ways
Who believes our Lord would speak a lie.
He promised faithfully your lives to raise
Though fate decreed your flesh should die;
His words as nonsense ye appraise
Who approve of naught not seen with eye;
And that presumption doth imply,
Which all good men doth ill beseem,
On tale as true ne'er to rely
Save private reason right it deem.

27 Do you deem that you yourself maintain
Such words as man to God should dare?
You will dwell, you say, in this domain:
'Twere best for leave first offer prayer,
And yet that grace you might not gain.
Now over this water you wish to fare:
By another course you must that attain;
Your flesh shall in clay find colder lair,
For our heedless father did of old prepare
Its doom by Eden's grove and stream;
Through dismal death must each man fare,
Ere o'er this deep him God redeem.'

28 'If my doom you deem it, maiden sweet,
  To mourn once more, then I must pine.
  Now my lost one found again I greet,
  Must bereavement new till death be mine?
  Why must I at once both part and meet?
  My precious pearl doth my pain design!
  What use hath treasure but tears to repeat,
  When one at its loss must again repine?
  Now I care not though my days decline
  Outlawed afar o'er land and stream;
  When in my pearl no part is mine,
  Only endless dolour one that may deem.'

29 'But of woe, I deem, and deep distress
  You speak,' she said. 'Why do you so?
  Through loud lament when they lose the less
  Oft many men the more forgo.
  'Twere better with cross yourself to bless,
  Ever praising God in weal and woe;
  For resentment gains you not a cress:
  Who must needs endure, he may not say no!
  For though you dance as any doe,
  Rampant bray or raging scream,
  When escape you cannot, to nor fro,
  His doom you must abide, I deem.

30 Deem God unjust, the Lord indict,
  From his way a foot He will not wend;
  The relief amounts not to a mite,
  Though gladness your grief may never end.
  Cease then to wrangle, to speak in spite,
  And swiftly seek Him as your friend.

Your prayer His pity may excite,
So that Mercy shall her powers expend.
To your languor He may comfort lend,
And swiftly your griefs removed may seem;
For lament or rave, to submit pretend,
'Tis His to ordain what He right may deem.'

31 THEN I said, I deem, to that damosel:
       'May I give no grievance to my Lord,
Rash fool, though blundering tale I tell.
My heart the pain of loss outpoured,
Gushing as water springs from well.
I commit me ever to His mercy's ward.
Rebuke me not with words so fell,
Though I erring stray, my dear adored!
But your comfort kindly to me accord,
In pity bethinking you of this:
For partner you did me pain award
On whom was founded all my bliss.

32 Both bliss and grief you have been to me,
But of woe far greater hath been my share.
You were caught away from all perils free,
But my pearl was gone, I knew not where;
My sorrow is softened now I it see.
When we parted, too, at one we were;
Now God forbid that we angry be!
We meet on our roads by chance so rare.
Though your converse courtly is and fair,
I am but mould and good manners miss.
Christ's mercy, Mary and John: I dare
Only on these to found my bliss.

33   In bliss you abide and happiness,
     And I with woe am worn and grey;
     Oft searing sorrows I possess,
     Yet little heed to that you pay.
     But now I here yourself address,
     Without reproach I would you pray
     To deign in sober words express
     What life you lead the livelong day.
     For delighted I am that your lot, you say,
     So glorious and so glad now is;
     There finds my joy its foremost way,
     On that is founded all my bliss.'

34   'Now bliss you ever bless!' she cried,
     Lovely in limb, in hue so clear,
     'And welcome here to walk and bide;
     For now your words are to me dear.
     Masterful mood and haughty pride,
     I warn you, are bitterly hated here.
     It doth not delight my Lord to chide,
     For meek are all that dwell Him near.
     So, when in His place you must appear,
     Be devout in humble lowliness:
     To my Lord, the Lamb, such a mien is dear,
     On whom is founded all my bliss.

35   A blissful life you say is mine;
     You wish to know in what degree.
     Your pearl you know you did resign
     When in young and tender years was she;
     Yet my Lord, the Lamb, through power divine
     Myself He chose His bride to be,

And crowned me queen in bliss to shine,
While days shall endure eternally.
Dowered with His heritage all is she
That is His love. I am wholly His:
On His glory, honour, and high degree
Are built and founded all my bliss.'

36   'O Blissful!' said I, 'can this be true?
     Be not displeased if in speech I err!
Are you the queen of heavens blue,
Whom all must honour on earth that fare?
We believe that our Grace of Mary grew,
Who in virgin-bloom a babe did bear;
And claim her crown: who could this do
But once that surpassed her in favour fair?
And yet for unrivalled sweetness rare
We call her the Phoenix of Araby,
That her Maker let faultless wing the air,
Like to the Queen of Courtesy.'

37   'O courteous Queen', that damsel said.
Kneeling on earth with uplifted face,
'Mother immaculate, and fairest maid,
Blessed beginner of every grace!'
Uprising then her prayer she stayed,
And there she spoke to me a space:
'Here many the prize they have gained are paid,
But usurpers, sir, here have no place.
That empress' realm doth heaven embrace,
And earth and hell she holds in fee,
From their heritage yet will none displace,
For she is the Queen of Courtesy.

38 The court where the living God doth reign
   Hath a virtue of its own being,
   That each who may thereto attain
   Of all the realm is queen or king,
   Yet never shall other's right obtain,
   But in other's good each glorying
   And wishing each crown worth five again,
   If amended might be so fair a thing.
   But my Lady of whom did Jesu spring,
   O'er us high she holds her empery,
   And none that grieves of our following,
   For she is the Queen of Courtesy.

39 In courtesy we are members all
   Of Jesus Christ, Saint Paul doth write:
   As head, arm, leg, and navel small
   To their body doth loyalty true unite,
   So as limbs to their Master mystical
   All Christian souls belong by right.
   Now among your limbs can you find at all
   Any tie or bond of hate or spite?
   Your head doth not feel affront or slight
   On your arm or finger though ring it see;
   So we all proceed in love's delight
   To king and queen by courtesy.'

40 'Courtesy,' I said, 'I do believe
   And charity great dwells you among,
   But may my words no wise you grieve,
   ....
   You in heaven too high yourself conceive
   To make you a queen who were so young.

What honour more might he achieve
Who in strife on earth was ever strong,
And lived his life in penance long
With his body's pain to get bliss for fee?
What greater glory could to him belong
Than king to be crowned by courtesy?

41 THAT courtesy gives its gifts too free,
    If it be sooth that you now say.
Two years you lived not on earth with me,
And God you could not please, nor pray
With Pater and Creed upon your knee –
And made a queen that very day!
I cannot believe, God helping me,
That God so far from right would stray.
Of a countess, damsel, I must say,
'Twere fair in heaven to find the grace,
Or of lady even of less array,
But a queen! It is too high a place.'

42 'Neither time nor place His grace confine',
Then said to me that maiden bright,
'For just is all that He doth assign,
And nothing can He work but right.
In God's true gospel, in words divine
That Matthew in your mass doth cite,
A tale he aptly doth design,
In parable saith of heaven's light:
"My realm on high I liken might
To a vineyard owner in this case.
The year had run to season right;
To dress the vines 'twas time and place.

43 All labourers know when that time is due.
　　The master up full early rose
　　To hire him vineyard workers new;
　　And some to suit his needs he chose.
　　Together they pledge agreement true
　　For a penny a day, and forth each goes,
　　Travails and toils to tie and hew,
　　Binds and prunes and in order stows.
　　In forenoon the master to market goes,
　　And there finds men that idle laze.
　　'Why stand ye idle?' he said to those.
　　'Do ye know not time of day nor place?'

44 'This place we reached betimes ere day',
　　This answer from all alike he drew,
　　'Since sunrise standing here we stay,
　　And no man offers us work to do.'
　　'Go to my vineyard! Do what ye may!'
　　Said the lord, and made a bargain true:
　　'In deed and intent I to you will pay
　　What hire may justly by night accrue.'
　　They went to his vines and laboured too,
　　But the lord all day that way did pace,
　　And brought to his vineyard workers new,
　　Till daytime almost passed that place.

45 In that place at time of evensong,
　　One hour before the set of sun,
　　He saw there idle labourers strong
　　And thus his earnest words did run:
　　'Why stand ye idle all day long?'
　　They said they chance of hire had none.

'Go to my vineyard, yeomen young,
And work and do what may be done!'
The hour grew late and sank the sun,
Dusk came o'er the world apace;
He called them to claim the wage they had won,
For time of day had passed that place.

46   THE time in that place he well did know;
     He called: 'Sir steward, the people pay!
Give them the hire that I them owe.
Moreover, that none reproach me may,
Set them all in a single row,
And to each alike give a penny a day;
Begin at the last that stands below,
Till to the first you make your way.'
Then the first began to complain and say
That they had laboured long and sore:
'These but one hour in stress did stay;
It seems to us we should get more.

47   More have we earned, we think it true,
Who have borne the daylong heat indeed,
Than these who hours have worked not two,
And yet you our equals have decreed.'
One such the lord then turned him to:
'My friend, I will not curtail your meed.
Go now and take what is your due!
For a penny I hired you as agreed,
Why now to wrangle do you proceed?
Was it not a penny you bargained for?
To surpass his bargain may no man plead.
Why then will you ask for more?

48 Nay, more – am I not allowed in gift
To dispose of mine as I please to do?
Or your eye to evil, maybe, you lift,
For I none betray and I am true?'
"Thus I", said Christ, "shall the order shift:
The last shall come first to take his due,
And the first come last, be he never so swift;
For many are called, but the favourites few."
Thus the poor get ever their portion too,
Though late they came and little bore;
And though to their labour little accrue,
The mercy of God is much the more.

49 More is my joy and bliss herein,
The flower of my life, my lady's height,
Than all the folk in the world might win,
Did they seek award on ground of right.
Though 'twas but now that I entered in,
And came to the vineyard by evening's light.
First with my hire did my Lord begin;
I was paid at once to the furthest mite.
Yet others in toil without respite
That had laboured and sweated long of yore,
He did not yet with hire requite,
Nor will, perchance, for years yet more.'

50 Then more I said and spoke out plain:
'Unreasonable is what you say.
Ever ready God's justice on high doth reign,
Or a fable doth Holy Writ purvey.
The Psalms a cogent verse contain,
Which puts a point that one must weigh:

"High King, who all dost foreordain,
His deserts Thou dost to each repay."
Now if daylong one did steadfast stay,
And you to payment came him before,
Then lesser work can earn more pay;
And the longer you reckon, the less hath more.'

51 'OF more and less in God's domains
        No question arises', said that maid,
'For equal hire there each one gains,
Be guerdon great or small him paid.
No churl is our Chieftain that in bounty reigns,
Be soft or hard by Him purveyed;
As water of dike His gifts He drains,
Or streams from a deep by drought unstayed.
Free is the pardon to him conveyed
Who in fear to the Saviour in sin did bow;
No bars from bliss will for such be made,
For the grace of God is great enow.

52 But now to defeat me you debate
That wrongly my penny I have taken here;
You say that I who came too late
Deserve not hire at price so dear.
Where heard you ever of man relate
Who, pious in prayer from year to year,
Did not somehow forfeit the guerdon great
Sometime of Heaven's glory clear?
Nay, wrong men work, from right they veer,
And ever the ofter the older, I trow.
Mercy and grace must then them steer,
For the grace of God is great enow.

53   But enow have the innocent of grace.
      As soon as born, in lawful line
      Baptismal waters them embrace;
      Then they are brought unto the vine.
      Anon the day with darkened face
      Doth toward the night of death decline.
      They wrought no wrong while in that place,
      And his workmen then pays the Lord divine.
      They were there; they worked at his design;
      Why should He not their toil allow,
      Yea, first to them their hire assign?
      For the grace of God is great enow.

54   Enow 'tis known that Man's high kind
      At first for perfect bliss was bred.
      Our eldest father that grace resigned
      Through an apple upon which he fed.
      We were all damned, for that food assigned
      To die in grief, all joy to shed,
      And after in flames of hell confined
      To dwell for ever unréspited.
      But soon a healing hither sped:
      Rich blood ran on rough rood-bough,
      And water fair. In that hour of dread
      The grace of God grew great enow.

55   Enow there went forth from that well
      Water and blood from wounds so wide:
      The blood redeemed us from pains of hell,
      Of the second death the bond untied;
      The water is baptism, truth to tell,
      That the spear so grimly ground let glide.

It washes away the trespass fell
By which Adam drowned us in deathly tide.
No bars in the world us from Bliss divide
In blessed hour restored, I trow,
Save those that He hath drawn aside;
And the grace of God is great enow.

56 GRACE enow may the man receive
Who sins anew, if he repent;
But craving it he must sigh and grieve
And abide what pains are consequent.
But reason that right can never leave
Evermore preserves the innocent;
'Tis a judgement God did never give
That the guiltless should ever have punishment.
The guilty, contrite and penitent,
Through mercy may to grace take flight;
But he that to treachery never bent
In innocence is saved by right.

57 It is right thus by reason, as in this case
I learn, to save these two from ill;
The righteous man shall see His face,
Come unto him the harmless will.
This point the Psalms in a passage raise:
'Who, Lord, shall climb Thy lofty hill,
Or rest within Thy holy place?"
He doth the answer swift fulfil:
"Who wrought with hands no harm nor ill,
Who is of heart both clean and bright,
His steps shall there be steadfast still":
The innocent ever is saved by right.

58 The righteous too, one many maintain,
   He shall to that noble tower repair,
   Who leads not his life in folly vain,
   Nor guilefully doth to neighbour swear.
   That Wisdom did honour once obtain
   For such doth Solomon declare:
   She pressed him on by ways made plain
   And showed him afar God's kingdom fair,
   As if saying: "That lovely island there
   That mayst thou win, be thou brave in fight."
   But to say this doubtless one may dare:
   The innocent ever is saved by right.

59 To righteous men – have you seen it there? –
   In the Psalter David a verse applied:
   "Do not, Lord, Thy servant to judgement bear;
   For to Thee none living is justified."
   So when to that Court you must repair
   Where all our cases shall be tried,
   If on right you stand, lest you trip beware,
   Warned by these words that I espied.
   But He on rood that bleeding died,
   Whose hands the nails did harshly smite,
   Grant you may pass, when you are tried,
   By innocence and not by right.

60 Let him that can rightly read in lore,
   Look in the Book and learn thereby
   How Jesus walked the world of yore,
   And people pressed their babes Him nigh,
   For joy and health from Him did pour.
   "Our children touch!" they humbly cry.

"Let be!" his disciples rebuked them sore,
And to many would approach deny.
Then Jesus sweetly did reply:
"Nay! let children by me alight;
For such is heaven prepared on high!"
The innocent ever is saved by right.

61 THEN Jesus summoned his servants mild,
And said His realm no man might win,
Unless he came there as a child;
Else never should he come therein.
Harmless, true, and undefiled,
Without mark or mar of soiling sin,
When such knock at those portals piled,
Quick for them men will the gate unpin.
That bliss unending dwells therein
That the jeweller sought, above gems did rate,
And sold all he had to clothe him in,
To purchase a pearl immaculate.

62 This pearl immaculate purchased dear
The jeweller gave all his goods to gain
Is like the realm of heaven's sphere:
So said the Lord of land and main;
For it is flawless, clean and clear,
Endlessly round, doth joy contain,
And is shared by all the righteous here.
Lo! amid my breast it doth remain;
There my Lord, the Lamb that was bleeding slain,
In token of peace it placed in state.
I bid you the wayward world disdain
And procure your pearl immaculate!'

63 'Immaculate Pearl in pearls unstained,
   Who bear of precious pearls the prize,
   Your figure fair for you who feigned?
   Who wrought your robe, he was full wise!
   Your beauty was never from nature gained;
   Pygmalion did ne'er your face devise;
   In Aristotle's learning is contained
   Of these properties' nature no surmise;
   Your hue the flower-de-luce defies,
   Your angel-bearing is of grace so great.
   What office, purest, me apprise
   Doth bear this pearl immaculate?'

64 'My immaculate Lamb, my final end
   Beloved, Who all can heal', said she,
   'Chose me as spouse, did to bridal bend
   That once would have seemed unmeet to be.
   From your weeping world when I did wend
   He called me to his felicity:
   "Come hither to me, sweetest friend,
   For no blot nor spot is found in thee!"
   Power and beauty he gave to me;
   In his blood he washed my weeds in state,
   Crowned me clean in virginity,
   And arrayed me in pearls immaculate.'

65 'Why, immaculate bride of brightest flame,
   Who royalty have so rich and rare,
   Of what kind can He be, the Lamb you name,
   Who would you His wedded wife declare?
   Over others all hath climbed your fame,
   In lady's life with Him to fare.

For Christ have lived in care and blame
Many comely maids with comb in hair;
Yet the prize from all those brave you bear,
And all debar from bridal state,
All save yourself so proud and fair,
A matchless maid immaculate.'

66 'IMMACULATE, without a stain,
    Flawless I am', said that fair queen;
'And that I may with grace maintain,
But "matchless" I said not nor do mean.
As brides of the Lamb in bliss we reign,
Twelve times twelve thousand strong, I ween,
As Apocalypse reveals it plain:
In a throng they there by John were seen;
On Zion's hill, that mount serene,
The apostle had dream divine of them
On that summit for marriage robed all clean
In the city of New Jerusalem.

67 Of Jerusalem my tale doth tell,
If you will know what His nature be,
My Lamb, my Lord, my dear Jewel,
My Joy, my Bliss, my Truelove free.
Isaiah the prophet once said well
In pity for His humility:
"That glorious Guiltless they did fell
Without cause or charge of felony,
As sheep to the slaughter led was He,
And as lamb the shearer in hand doth hem
His mouth he closed without plaint or plea,
When the Jews Him judged in Jerusalem."

68 In Jerusalem was my Truelove slain,
    On the rood by ruffians fierce was rent;
    Willing to suffer all our pain
    To Himself our sorrows sad He lent.
    With cruel blows His face was flain
    That was to behold so excellent:
    He for sin to be set at naught did deign,
    Who of sin Himself was innocent.
    Beneath the scourge and thorns He bent,
    And stretched on a cross's brutal stem
    As meek as lamb made no lament,
    And died for us in Jerusalem.

69 In Jerusalem, Jordan, and Galilee,
    As there baptized the good Saint John,
    With Isaiah well did his words agree.
    When to meet him once had Jesus gone
    He spake of Him this prophecy:
    "Lo, the Lamb of God whom our trust is on!
    From the grievous sins He sets us free
    That all this world hath daily done."
    He wrought himself yet never one,
    Though He smirched himself with all of them.
    Who can tell the Fathering of that Son
    That died for us in Jerusalem?

70 In Jerusalem as lamb they knew
    And twice thus took my Truelove dear,
    As in prophets both is record true,
    For His meekness and His gentle cheer.
    The third time well is matched thereto,
    In Apocalypse 'tis written clear:

Where sat the saints, Him clear to view
Amidst the throne the Apostle dear
Saw loose the leaves of the book and shear
The seven signets sewn on them.
At that sight all folk there bowed in fear
In hell, in earth, and Jerusalem.

71 JERUSALEM'S Lamb had never stain
Of other hue than whiteness fair;
There blot nor blemish could remain,
So white the wool, so rich and rare.
Thus every soul that no soil did gain
His comely wife doth the Lamb declare;
Though each day He a host obtain,
No grudge nor grievance do we bear,
But for each one five we wish there were.
The more the merrier, so God me bless!
Our love doth thrive where many fare
In honour more and never less.

72 To less of bliss may none us bring
Who bear this pearl upon each breast,
For ne'er could they think of quarrelling
Of spotless pearls who bear the crest.
Though the clods may to our corses cling,
And for woe ye wail bereaved of rest,
From one death all our trust doth spring
In knowledge complete by us possessed.
The Lamb us gladdens, and, our grief redressed,
Doth at every Mass with joy us bless.
Here each hath bliss supreme and best,
Yet no one's honour is ever the less.

73 Lest less to trust my tale you hold,
In Apocalypse 'tis writ somewhere:
"The Lamb", saith John, "I could behold
On Zion standing proud and fair;
With him maidens a hundred-thousand fold,
And four and forty thousand were,
Who all upon their brows inscrolled
The Lamb's name and His Father's bare.
A shout then I heard from heaven there,
Like many floods met in pouring press;
And as thunder in darkling tors doth blare,
That noise, I believe, was nowise less.

74 But nonetheless, though it harshly roared,
And echo loud though it was to hear,
I heard them note then new record,
A delight as lovely to listening ear
As harpers harping on harps afford.
This new song now they sang full clear,
With resounding notes in noble accord
Making in choir their musics dear.
Before God's very throne drawn near
And the Beasts to Him bowed in lowliness
And the ancient Elders grave of cheer
They sang their song there, nonetheless.

75 Yet nonetheless were none so wise
For all the arts that they ever knew
Of that song who could a phrase devise,
Save those of the Lamb's fair retinue;
For redeemed and removed from earthly eyes,
As firstling fruits that to God are due,

To the noble Lamb they are allies,
Being like to Him in mien and hue;
For no lying word nor tale untrue
Ever touched their tongues despite duress.
Ever close that company pure shall sue
That Master immaculate, and never less.'"

76 'My thanks may none the less you find,
My Pearl', quoth I, 'though I question pose.
I should not try your lofty mind,
Whom Christ to bridal chamber chose.
I am but dirt and dust in kind,
And you a rich and radiant rose
Here by this blissful bank reclined
Where life's delight unfading grows.
Now, Lady, your heart sincere enclose,
And I would ask one thing express,
And though it clown uncouth me shows,
My prayer disdain not, nevertheless.

77 I NONETHELESS my appeal declare,
If you to do this may well deign,
Deny you not my piteous prayer,
As you are glorious without a stain.
No home in castle-wall do ye share,
No mansion to meet in, no domain?
Of Jerusalem you speak the royal and fair,
Where David on regal throne did reign;
It abides not here on hill nor plain,
But in Judah is that noble plot.
As under moon ye have no stain
Your home should be without a spot.

78   This spotless troop of which you tell,
     This thronging press many-thousandfold,
     Ye doubtless a mighty citadel
     Must have your number great to hold:
     For jewels so lovely 'twould not be well
     That flock so fair should have no fold!
     Yet by these banks where a while I dwell
     I nowhere about any house behold.
     To gaze on this glorious stream you strolled
     And linger alone now, do you not?
     If elsewhere you have stout stronghold,
     Now guide me to that goodly spot!'

79   'That spot', that peerless maid replied,
     'In Judah's land of which you spake,
     Is the city to which the Lamb did ride,
     To suffer sore there for Man's sake.
     The Old Jerusalem is implied,
     For old sin's bond He there let break.
     But the New, that God sent down to glide,
     The Apocalypse in account doth take.
     The Lamb that no blot ever black shall make
     Doth there His lovely throng allot,
     And as His flock all stains forsake
     So His mansion is unmarred by spot.

80   There are two spots. To speak of these:
     They both the name "Jerusalem" share;
     "The City of God" or "Sight of Peace",
     These meanings only doth that bear.
     In the first it once the Lamb did please
     Our peace by His suffering to repair;

In the other naught is found but peace
That shall last for ever without impair.
To that high city we swiftly fare
As soon as our flesh is laid to rot;
Ever grow shall the bliss and glory there
For the host within that hath no spot.'

81 'O spotless maiden kind!' I cried
To that lovely flower, 'O lead me there,
To see where blissful you abide,
To that goodly place let me repair!'
'God will forbid that', she replied,
'His tower to enter you may not dare.
But the Lamb hath leave to me supplied
For a sight thereof by favour rare:
From without on that precinct pure to stare,
But foot within to venture not;
In the street you have no strength to fare,
Unless clean you be without a spot.

82 IF I this spot shall to you unhide,
Turn up towards this water's head,
While I escort you on this side,
Until your ways to a hill have led.'
No longer would I then abide,
But shrouded by leafy boughs did tread,
Until from a hill I there espied
A glimpse of that city, as forth I sped.
Beyond the river below me spread
Brighter than sun with beams it shone;
In the Apocalypse may its form be read,
As it describes the apostle John.

83   As John the apostle it did view,
    I saw that city of great renown,
    Jerusalem royally arrayed and new,
    As it was drawn from heaven down.
    Of gold refined in fire to hue
    Of glittering glass was that shining town;
    Fair gems beneath were joined as due
    In courses twelve, on the base laid down
    That with tenoned tables twelve they crown:
    A single stone was each tier thereon,
    As well describes this wondrous town
    In apocalypse the apostle John.

84   These stones doth John in Writ disclose;
    I knew their names as he doth tell:
    As jewel first the jasper rose,
    And first at the base I saw it well,
    On the lowest course it greenly glows;
    On the second stage doth sapphire dwell;
    Chalcedony on the third tier shows,
    A flawless, pure, and pale jewel;
    The emerald fourth so green of shell;
    The sardonyx, the fifth it shone,
    The ruby sixth: he saw it well
    In the Apocalypse, the apostle John.

85   To them John then joined the chrysolite,
    The seventh gem in the ascent;
    The eighth the beryl clear and white;
    The twin-hued topaz as ninth was pent;
    Tenth the chrysoprase formed the flight;
    Eleventh was jacinth excellent;

The twelfth, most trusty in every plight,
The amethyst blue with purple blent.
Sheer from those tiers the wall then went
Of jasper like glass that glistening shone;
I knew it, for thus did it present
In the Apocalypse the apostle John.

86 As John described, I broad and sheer
These twelve degrees saw rising there;
Above the city square did rear
(Its length with breadth and height compare);
The streets of gold as glass all clear,
The wall of jasper that gleamed like glair;
With all precious stones that might there appear
Adorned within the dwellings were.
Of that domain each side all square
Twelve thousand furlongs held then on,
As in height and breadth, in length did fare,
For it measured saw the apostle John.

87 As John hath writ, I saw yet more:
Each quadrate wall there had three gates,
So in compass there were three times four,
The portals o'erlaid with richest plates;
A single pearl was every door,
A pearl whose perfection ne'er abates;
And each inscribed a name there bore
Of Israel's children by their dates:
Their times of birth each allocates,
Ever first the eldest thereon is hewn.
Such light every street illuminates
They have need of neither sun nor moon.

88 Of sun nor moon they had no need,
For God Himself was their sunlight;
The Lamb their lantern was indeed
And through Him blazed that city bright
That unearthly clear did no light impede;
Through wall and hall thus passed my sight.
The Throne on high there might one heed,
With all its rich adornment dight,
As John in chosen words did write.
High God Himself sat on that throne,
Whence forth a river ran with light
Outshining both the sun and moon.

89 Neither sun nor moon ever shone so sweet
As the pouring flood from that court that flowed;
Swiftly it swept through every street,
And no filth nor soil nor slime it showed.
No church was there the sight to greet,
Nor chapel nor temple there ever abode:
The Almighty was their minster meet;
Refreshment the Victim Lamb bestowed.
The gates ever open to every road
Were never yet shut from noon to noon;
There enters none to find abode
Who bears any spot beneath the moon.

90 The moon therefrom may gain no might,
Too spotty is she, of form too hoar;
Moreover there comes never night:
Why should the moon in circle soar
And compare her with that peerless light
That shines upon that water's shore?

The planets are in too poor a plight,
Yea, the sun himself too pale and frore.
On shining trees where those waters pour
Twelve fruits of life there ripen soon;
Twelve times a year they bear a store,
And renew them anew in every moon.

91   Such marvels as neath the moon upraised
A fleshly heart could not endure
I saw, who on that castle gazed;
Such wonders did its frame immure,
I stood there still as quail all dazed;
Its wondrous form did me allure,
That rest nor toil I felt, amazed,
And ravished by that radiance pure.
For with conscience clear I you assure,
If man embodied had gained that boon,
Though sages all assayed his cure,
His life had been lost beneath the moon.

92   As doth the moon in might arise,
Ere down must daylight leave the air,
So, suddenly, in a wondrous wise,
Of procession long I was aware.
Unheralded to my surprise
That city of royal renown so fair
Was with virgins filled in the very guise
Of my blissful one with crown on hair.
All crowned in manner like they were,
In pearls appointed, and weeds of white,
And bound on breast did each one bear
The blissful pearl with great delight.

93 With great delight in line they strolled
  On golden ways that gleamed like glass;
  A hundred thousands were there, I hold,
  And all to match their livery was;
  The gladdest face could none have told.
  The Lamb before did proudly pass
  With seven horns of clear red gold;
  As pearls of price His raiment was.
  To the Throne now drawn they pacing pass:
  No crowding, though great their host in white,
  But gentle as modest maids at Mass,
  So lead they on with great delight.

94 The delight too great were to recall
  That at His coming forth did swell.
  When He approached those elders all
  On their faces at His feet they fell;
  There summoned hosts angelical
  An incense cast of sweetest smell:
  New glory and joy then forth did fall,
  All sang to praise that fair Jewel.
  The strain could strike through earth to hell
  That the Virtues of heaven in joy endite.
  With His host to laud the Lamb as well
  Indeed I found a great delight.

95 Delight the Lamb to behold with eyes
  Then moved my mind with wonder more:
  The best was He, blithest, most dear to prize
  Of whom I e'er heard tales of yore;
  So wondrous white was all His guise,
  So noble Himself He so meekly bore.

But by His heart a wound my eyes
Saw wide and wet; the fleece it tore,
From His white side His blood did pour.
Alas! thought I, who did that spite?
His breast should have burned with anguish sore,
Ere in that deed one took delight.

96 The Lamb's delight to doubt, I ween,
None wished; though wound He sore displayed,
In His face no sign thereof was seen,
In His glance such glorious gladness played.
I marked among His host serene,
How life in full on each was laid –
Then saw I there my little queen
That I thought stood by me in the glade!
Lord! great was the merriment she made,
Among her peers who was so white.
That vision made me think to wade
For love-longing in great delight.

97 DELIGHT there pierced my eye and ear,
In my mortal mind a madness reigned;
When I saw her beauty I would be near,
Though beyond the stream she was retained.
I thought that naught could interfere,
Could strike me back to halt constrained,
From plunge in stream would none me steer,
Though I died ere I swam o'er what remained.
But as wild in the water to start I strained,
On my intent did quaking seize;
From that aim recalled I was detained:
It was not as my Prince did please.

98 It pleased Him not that I leapt o'er
    Those marvellous bounds by madness swayed.
    Though headlong haste me heedless bore,
    Yet swift arrest was on me made,
    For right as I rushed then to the shore
    That fury made my dream to fade.
    I woke in that garden as before,
    My head upon that mound was laid
    Where once to earth my pearl had strayed.
    I stretched, and fell in great unease,
    And sighing to myself I prayed:
    'Now all be as that Prince may please.'

99 It pleased me ill outcast to be
    So suddenly from that region fair
    Where living beauty I could see.
    A swoon of longing smote me there,
    And I cried aloud then piteously:
    'O Pearl, renowned beyond compare!
    How dear was all that you said to me,
    That vision true while I did share.
    If it be true and sooth to swear
    That in garland gay you are set at ease,
    Then happy I, though chained in care,
    That you that Prince indeed do please.'

100 To please that Prince had I always bent,
    Desired no more than was my share,
    And loyally been obedient,
    As the Pearl me prayed so debonair,
    I before God's face might have been sent,
    In his mysteries further maybe to fare.
    But with fortune no man is content

That rightly he may claim and bear;
So robbed of realms immortally fair
Too soon my joy did sorrow seize.
Lord! mad are they who against Thee dare
Or purpose what Thee may displease!

101 To please that Prince, or be pardon shown,
May Christian good with ease design;
For day and night I have him known
A God, a Lord, a Friend divine.
This chance I met on mound where prone
In grief for my pearl I would repine;
With Christ's sweet blessing and mine own
I then to God it did resign.
May He that in form of bread and wine
By priest upheld each day one sees,
Us inmates of His house divine
Make precious pearls Himself to please.   *Amen Amen*

Sir Orfeo

S*ir Orfeo* is found in three manuscripts, of which the earliest gives very much the best text; this is the Auchinleck manuscript, a large miscellany made about 1330, probably in London, and now in the Advocates' Library in Edinburgh. The other manuscripts, both of the fifteenth century, offer very decrepit versions of the poem; but the Auchinleck text has also suffered from the corruptions of error and forgetfulness, if much less so than the others. The translation follows the Auchinleck text (with some emendations), except at the beginning, where a leaf is lost from the manuscript. Auchinleck begins with *Orfeo was a king* (line 25 of the translation); but the manuscript Harley 3810 precedes this with the 24-line prologue which is here translated. This prologue appears also in a very corrupt state in the third manuscript, Ashmole 61; and, remarkably, also elsewhere in the Auchinleck manuscript, as the prologue of another poem, *Lay le Freyne*, which has been thought to be the work of the same author. In addition, lines 33-46 in the translation are introduced from the Harley manuscript; they are agreed to be genuine lines of the original. It is agreed that the references to England (line 26) and to Winchester (lines 49–50, and line 478), which are peculiar to the Auchinleck version, are not authentic.

It cannot be said where or when *Sir Orfeo* was composed with any more precision than probably in the south-east of

England in the latter part of the thirteenth century, or early in the fourteenth; and it seems at any rate more probable than not that it was translated from a French original.

WE often read and written find,
    as learned men do us remind,
that lays that now the harpers sing
are wrought of many a marvellous thing.
Some are of weal, and some of woe,
and some do joy and gladness know;
in some are guile and treachery told,
in some the deeds that chanced of old;
some are of jests and ribaldry,
10   and some are tales of Faërie.
Of all the things that men may heed
'tis most of love they sing indeed.
    In Britain all these lays are writ,
there issued first in rhyming fit,
concerning adventures in those days
whereof the Britons made their lays;
for when they heard men anywhere
tell of adventures that there were,
they took their harps in their delight
20   and made a lay and named it right.
    Of adventures that did once befall
some can I tell you, but not all.
Listen now, lordings good and true,
and 'Orfeo' I will sing to you.

Sir Orfeo was a king of old,
in England lordship high did hold;
valour he had and hardihood,
a courteous king whose gifts were good.
His father from King Pluto came,
30   his mother from Juno, king of fame,
who once of old as gods were named
for mighty deeds they did and claimed.
Sir Orfeo, too, all things beyond
of harping's sweet delight was fond,
and sure were all good harpers there
of him to earn them honour fair;
himself he loved to touch the harp
and pluck the strings with fingers sharp.
He played so well, beneath the sun
40   a better harper was there none;
no man hath in this world been born
who would not, hearing him, have sworn
that as before him Orfeo played
to joy of Paradise he had strayed
and sound of harpers heavenly,
such joy was there and melody.
This king abode in Tracience,
a city proud of stout defence;
for Winchester, 'tis certain, then
50   as Tracience was known to men.
There dwelt his queen in fairest bliss,
whom men called Lady Heurodis,
of ladies then the one most fair
who ever flesh and blood did wear;
in her did grace and goodness dwell,
but none her loveliness can tell.

*

It so did chance in early May,
when glad and warm doth shine the day,
and gone are bitter winter showers,
60   and every field is filled with flowers,
on every branch the blossom blows,
in glory and in gladness grows,
the lady Heurodis, the queen,
two maidens fair to garden green
with her she took at drowsy tide
of noon to stroll by orchard-side,
to see the flowers there spread and spring
and hear the birds on branches sing.
    There down in shade they sat all three
70   beneath a fair young grafted tree;
and soon it chanced the gentle queen
fell there asleep upon the green.
Her maidens durst her not awake,
but let her lie, her rest to take;
and so she slept, till midday soon
was passed, and come was afternoon.
Then suddenly they heard her wake,
and cry, and grievous clamour make;
she writhed with limb, her hands she wrung,
80   she tore her face till blood there sprung,
her raiment rich in pieces rent;
thus sudden out of mind she went.
    Her maidens two then by her side
no longer durst with her abide,
but to the palace swiftly ran
and told there knight and squire and man
their queen, it seemed, was sudden mad;
'Go and restrain her,' they them bade.
Both knights and ladies thither sped,

90   and more than sixty damsels fled;
to the orchard to the queen they went,
with arms to lift her down they bent,
and brought her to her bed at last,
and raving there they held her fast;
but ceaselessly she still would cry,
and ever strove to rise and fly.

    When Orfeo heard these tidings sad,
more grief than ever in life he had;
and swiftly with ten knights he sped

100 to bower, and stood before her bed,
and looking on her ruefully,
'Dear life,' he said, 'what troubles thee,
who ever quiet hast been and sweet,
why dost thou now so shrilly greet?
Thy body that peerless white was born
is now by cruel nails all torn.
Alas! thy cheeks that were so red
are now as wan as thou wert dead;
thy fingers too, so small and slim,

110 are stained with blood, their hue is dim.
Alas! thy lovely eyes in woe
now stare on me as on a foe.
A! lady, mercy I implore.
These piteous cries, come, cry no more,
but tell me what thee grieves, and how,
and say what may thee comfort now.'

    Then, lo! at last she lay there still,
and many bitter tears did spill,
and thus unto the king she spake:

120 'Alas! my lord, my heart will break.
Since first together came our life,
between us ne'er was wrath nor strife,

but I have ever so loved thee
as very life, and so thou me.
Yet now we must be torn in twain,
and go I must, for all thy pain.'
    'Alas!' said he, 'then dark my doom.
Where wilt thou go, and go to whom?
But where thou goest, I come with thee,
130 and where I go, thou shalt with me.'
    'Nay, nay, sir, words avail thee naught.
I will tell thee how this woe was wrought:
as I lay in the quiet noontide
and slept beneath our orchard-side,
there came two noble knights to me
arrayed in armour gallantly.
"We come", they said, "thee swift to bring
to meeting with our lord and king."
Then answered I both bold and true
140 that dared I not, and would not do.
They spurred then back on swiftest steed;
then came their king himself with speed;
a hundred knights with him and more,
and damsels, too, were many a score,
all riding there on snow-white steeds,
and white as milk were all their weeds;
I saw not ever anywhere
a folk so peerless and so fair.
The king was crowned with crown of light,
150 not of red gold nor silver white,
but of one single gem 'twas hewn
that shone as bright as sun at noon.
And coming, straightway he me sought,
and would I or no, he up me caught,
and made me by him swiftly ride

upon a palfrey at his side;
and to his palace thus me brought,
a dwelling fair and wondrous wrought.
He castles showed me there and towers,
160 Water and wild, and woods, and flowers,
and pastures rich upon the plain;
and then he brought me home again,
and to our orchard he me led,
and then at parting this he said:
"See, lady, tomorrow thou must be
right here beneath this grafted tree,
and then beside us thou shalt ride,
and with us evermore abide.
If let or hindrance thou dost make,
170 where'er thou be, we shall thee take,
and all thy limbs shall rend and tear –
no aid of man shall help thee there;
and even so, all rent and torn,
thou shalt away with us be borne."'

When all those tidings Orfeo heard,
then spake he many a bitter word:
'Alas! I had liever lose my life
than lose thee thus, my queen and wife!'
He counsel sought of every man,
180 but none could find him help or plan.
On the morrow, when the noon drew near,
in arms did Orfeo appear,
and full ten hundred knights with him,
all stoutly armed, all stern and grim;
and with their queen now went that band
beneath the grafted tree to stand.
A serried rank on every side

they made, and vowed there to abide,
and die there sooner for her sake
190 than let men thence their lady take.
And yet from midst of that array
the queen was sudden snatched away;
by magic was she from them caught,
and none knew whither she was brought.

Then was there wailing, tears, and woe;
the king did to his chamber go,
and oft he swooned on floor of stone,
and such lament he made and moan
that nigh his life then came to end;
200 and nothing could his grief amend.
His barons he summoned to his board,
each mighty earl and famous lord,
and when they all together came,
'My lords,' he said, 'I here do name
my steward high before you all
to keep my realm, whate'er befall,
to hold my place instead of me
and keep my lands where'er they be.
For now that I have lost my queen,
210 the fairest lady men have seen,
I wish not woman more to see.
Into the wilderness I will flee,
and there will live for evermore
with the wild beasts in forests hoar.
But when ye learn my days are spent,
then summon ye a parliament,
and choose ye there a king anew.
With all I have now deal ye true.'

Then weeping was there in the hall,
220 and great lament there made they all,

and hardly there might old or young
for weeping utter word with tongue.
They knelt them down in company,
and prayed, if so his will might be,
that never should he from them go.
'Have done!' said he. 'It must be so.'

    Now all his kingdom he forsook.
Only a beggar's cloak he took;
he had no kirtle and no hood,
230 no shirt, nor other raiment good.
His harp yet bore he even so,
and barefoot from the gate did go;
no man might keep him on the way.
    A me! the weeping woe that day,
when he that had been king with crown
went thus beggarly out of town!
Through wood and over moorland bleak
he now the wilderness doth seek,
and nothing finds to make him glad,
240 but ever liveth lone and sad.
He once had ermine worn and vair,
on bed had purple linen fair,
now on the heather hard doth lie,
in leaves is wrapped and grasses dry.
He once had castles owned and towers,
water and wild, and woods, and flowers,
now though it turn to frost or snow,
this king with moss his bed must strow.
He once had many a noble knight
250 before him kneeling, ladies bright,
now nought to please him doth he keep;
only wild serpents by him creep.

He that once had in plenty sweet
all dainties for his drink and meat,
now he must grub and dig all day,
with roots his hunger to allay.
In summer on wildwood fruit he feeds,
or berries poor to serve his needs;
in winter nothing can he find
260 save roots and herbs and bitter rind.
All his body was wasted thin
by hardship, and all cracked his skin.
A Lord! who can recount the woe
for ten long years that king did know?
His hair and beard all black and rank
down to his waist hung long and lank.
His harp wherein was his delight
in hollow tree he hid from sight;
when weather clear was in the land
270 his harp he took then in his hand
and harped thereon at his sweet will.
Through all the wood the sound did thrill,
and all the wild beasts that there are
in joy approached him from afar;
and all the birds that might be found
there perched on bough and bramble round
to hear his harping to the end,
such melodies he there did blend;
and when he laid his harp aside,
280 no bird or beast would near him bide.

There often by him would he see,
when noon was hot on leaf and tree,
the king of Faërie with his rout
came hunting in the woods about

with blowing far and crying dim,
and barking hounds that were with him;
yet never a beast they took nor slew,
and where they went he never knew.
At other times he would descry
290 a mighty host, it seemed, go by,
ten hundred knights all fair arrayed
with many a banner proud displayed.
Each face and mien was fierce and bold,
each knight a drawn sword there did hold,
and all were armed in harness fair
and marching on he knew not where.
Or a sight more strange would meet his eye:
knights and ladies came dancing by
in rich array and raiment meet,
300 softly stepping with skilful feet;
tabour and trumpet went along,
and marvellous minstrelsy and song.

And one fair day he at his side
saw sixty ladies on horses ride,
each fair and free as bird on spray,
and never a man with them that day.
There each on hand a falcon bore,
riding a-hawking by river-shore.
Those haunts with game in plenty teem,
310 cormorant, heron, and duck in stream;
there off the water fowl arise,
and every falcon them descries;
each falcon stooping slew his prey,
and Orfeo laughing loud did say:
'Behold, in faith, this sport is fair!
Fore Heaven, I will betake me there!

I once was wont to see such play.'
He rose and thither made his way,
and to a lady came with speed,
320   and looked at her, and took good heed,
and saw as sure as once in life
'twas Heurodis, his queen and wife.
Intent he gazed, and so did she,
but no word spake; no word said he.
For hardship that she saw him bear,
who had been royal, and high, and fair,
then from her eyes the tears there fell.
The other ladies marked it well,
and away they made her swiftly ride;
330   no longer might she near him bide.
    'Alas!' said he, 'unhappy day!
Why will not now my death me slay?
Alas! unhappy man, ah why
may I not, seeing her, now die?
Alas! too long hath lasted life,
when I dare not with mine own wife
to speak a word, nor she with me.
Alas! my heart should break,' said he.
'And yet, fore Heaven, tide what betide,
340   and whithersoever these ladies ride,
that road I will follow they now fare;
for life or death no more I care.'
   His beggar's cloak he on him flung,
his harp upon his back he hung;
with right good will his feet he sped,
for stock nor stone he stayed his tread.
Right into a rock the ladies rode,
and in behind he fearless strode.
He went into that rocky hill

350　a good three miles or more, until
　　　he came into a country fair
　　　as bright as sun in summer air.
　　　Level and smooth it was and green,
　　　and hill nor valley there was seen.
　　　A castle he saw amid the land
　　　princely and proud and lofty stand;
　　　the outer wall around it laid
　　　of shining crystal clear was made.
　　　A hundred towers were raised about
360　with cunning wrought, embattled stout;
　　　and from the moat each buttress bold
　　　in arches sprang of rich red gold.
　　　The vault was carven and adorned
　　　with beasts and birds and figures horned;
　　　within were halls and chambers wide
　　　all made of jewels and gems of pride;
　　　the poorest pillar to behold
　　　was builded all of burnished gold.
　　　And all that land was ever light,
370　for when it came to dusk of night
　　　from precious stones there issued soon
　　　a light as bright as sun at noon.
　　　No man may tell nor think in thought
　　　how rich the works that there were wrought;
　　　indeed it seemed he gazed with eyes
　　　on the proud court of Paradise.
　　　　　The ladies to that castle passed.
　　　Behind them Orfeo followed fast.
　　　There knocked he loud upon the gate;
380　the porter came, and did not wait,
　　　but asked him what might be his will.
　　　'In faith, I have a minstrel's skill

with mirth and music, if he please,
thy lord to cheer, and him to ease.'
The porter swift did then unpin
the castle gates, and let him in.
    Then he began to gaze about,
and saw within the walls a rout
of folk that were thither drawn below,
390 and mourned as dead, but were not so.
For some there stood who had no head,
and some no arms, nor feet; some bled
and through their bodies wounds were set,
and some were strangled as they ate,
and some lay raving, chained and bound,
and some in water had been drowned;
and some were withered in the fire,
and some on horse, in war's attire,
and wives there lay in their childbed,
400 and mad were some, and some were dead;
and passing many there lay beside
as though they slept at quiet noon-tide.
Thus in the world was each one caught
and thither by fairy magic brought.
There too he saw his own sweet wife,
Queen Heurodis, his joy and life,
asleep beneath a grafted tree:
by her attire he knew 'twas she.
    When he had marked these marvels all,
410 he went before the king in hall,
and there a joyous sight did see,
a shining throne and canopy.
Their king and lord there held his seat
beside their lady fair and sweet.
Their crowns and clothes so brightly shone

that scarce his eyes might look thereon.
    When he had marked this wondrous thing,
he knelt him down before the king:
'O lord,' said he, 'if it be thy will,
420 now shalt thou hear my minstrel's skill.'
The king replied: 'What man art thou
that hither darest venture now?
Not I nor any here with me
have ever sent to summon thee,
and since here first my reign began
I have never found so rash a man
that he to us would dare to wend,
unless I first for him should send.'
'My lord,' said he, 'I thee assure,
430 I am but a wandering minstrel poor;
and, sir, this custom use we all
at the house of many a lord to call,
and little though our welcome be,
to offer there our minstrelsy.'
    Before the king upon the ground
he sat, and touched his harp to sound;
his harp he tuned as well he could,
glad notes began and music good,
and all who were in palace found
440 came unto him to hear the sound,
and lay before his very feet,
they thought his melody so sweet.
He played, and silent sat the king
for great delight in listening;
great joy this minstrelsy he deemed,
and joy to his noble queen it seemed.
    At last when he his harping stayed,
this speech the king to him then made:

'Minstrel, thy music pleaseth me.
450 Come, ask of me whate'er it be,
and rich reward I will thee pay.
Come, speak, and prove now what I say!'
'Good sir,' he said, 'I beg of thee
that this thing thou wouldst give to me,
that very lady fair to see
who sleeps beneath the grafted tree.'
'Nay,' said the king, 'that would not do!
A sorry pair ye'd make, ye two;
for thou art black, and rough, and lean,
460 and she is faultless, fair and clean.
A monstrous thing then would it be
to see her in thy company.'

   'O sir,' he said, 'O gracious king,
but it would be a fouler thing
from mouth of thine to hear a lie.
Thy vow, sir, thou canst not deny,
Whate'er I asked, that should I gain,
and thou must needs thy word maintain.'
The king then said: 'Since that is so,
470 now take her hand in thine, and go;
I wish thee joy of her, my friend!'

   He thanked him well, on knees did bend;
his wife he took then by the hand,
and departed swiftly from that land,
and from that country went in haste;
the way he came he now retraced.

   Long was the road. The journey passed;
to Winchester he came at last,
his own beloved city free;
480 but no man knew that it was he.
Beyond the town's end yet to fare,

lest men them knew, he did not dare;
but in a beggar's narrow cot
a lowly lodging there he got
both for himself and for his wife,
as a minstrel poor of wandering life.
He asked for tidings in the land,
and who that kingdom held in hand;
the beggar poor him answered well
490 and told all things that there befell:
how fairies stole their queen away
ten years before, in time of May;
and how in exile went their king
in unknown countries wandering,
while still the steward rule did hold;
and many things beside he told.

    Next day, when hour of noon was near,
he bade his wife await him here;
the beggar's rags he on him flung,
500 his harp upon his back he hung,
and went into the city's ways
for men to look and on him gaze.
Him earl and lord and baron bold,
lady and burgess, did behold.
'O look! O what a man!' they said,
'How long the hair hangs from his head!
His beard is dangling to his knee!
He is gnarled and knotted like a tree!'
    Then as he walked along the street
510 He chanced his steward there to meet,
and after him aloud cried he:
'Mercy, sir steward, have on me!
A harper I am from Heathenesse;
to thee I turn in my distress.'

The steward said: 'Come with me, come!
Of what I have thou shalt have some.
All harpers good I welcome make
For my dear lord Sir Orfeo's sake.'
  The steward in castle sat at meat,
520 and many a lord there had his seat;
trumpeters, tabourers there played
harpers and fiddlers music made.
Many a melody made they all,
but Orfeo silent sat in hall
and listened. And when they all were still
he took his harp and tuned it shrill.
Then notes he harped more glad and clear
than ever a man hath heard with ear;
his music delighted all those men.
530   The steward looked and looked again;
the harp in hand at once he knew.
'Minstrel,' he said, 'come, tell me true,
whence came this harp to thee, and how?
I pray thee, tell me plainly now.'
'My lord,' said he, 'in lands unknown
I walked a wilderness alone,
and there I found in dale forlorn
a man by lions to pieces torn,
by wolves devoured with teeth so sharp;
540 by him I found this very harp,
and that is full ten years ago.'
'Ah!' said the steward, 'news of woe!
'Twas Orfeo, my master true.
Alas! poor wretch, what shall I do,
who must so dear a master mourn?
A! woe is me that I was born,
for him so hard a fate designed,

a death so vile that he should find!'
Then on the ground he fell in swoon;
550 his barons stooping raised him soon
and bade him think how all must end –
for death of man no man can mend.

    King Orfeo now had proved and knew
his steward was both loyal and true,
and loved him as he duly should.
'Lo!' then he cried, and up he stood,
'Steward, now to my words give ear!
If thy king, Orfeo, were here,
and had in wilderness full long
560 suffered great hardship sore and strong,
had won his queen by his own hand
out of the deeps of fairy land,
and led at last his lady dear
right hither to the town's end near,
and lodged her in a beggar's cot;
if I were he, whom ye knew not,
thus come among you, poor and ill,
in secret to prove thy faith and will,
if then I thee had found so true,
570 thy loyalty never shouldst thou rue:
nay, certainly, tide what betide,
thou shouldst be king when Orfeo died.
Hadst thou rejoiced to hear my fate,
I would have thrust thee from the gate.'

    Then clearly knew they in the hall
that Orfeo stood before them all.
The steward understood at last;
in his haste the table down he cast
and flung himself before his feet,
580 and each lord likewise left his seat,

and this one cry they all let ring:
'Ye are our lord, sir, and our king!'
To know he lived so glad they were.
To his chamber soon they brought him there;
they bathed him and they shaved his beard,
and robed him, till royal he appeared;
and brought them in procession long
the queen to town with merry song,
with many a sound of minstrelsy.
590 A Lord! how great the melody!
For joy the tears were falling fast
of those who saw them safe at last.

    Now was King Orfeo crowned anew,
and Heurodis his lady too;
and long they lived, till they were dead,
and king was the steward in their stead.

    Harpers in Britain in aftertime
these marvels heard, and in their rhyme
a lay they made of fair delight,
600 and after the king it named aright,
'Orfeo' called it, as was meet:
good is the lay, the music sweet.

    Thus came Sir Orfeo out of care.
God grant that well we all may fare!

GLOSSARY

This glossary provides no more than the meanings of some archaic and technical words used in the translations, and only the meanings that the translator intended in those contexts (which in a very few cases may be doubtful). In the stanzas describing the breaking-up of the deer he employed some of the technical terms of the original which are debatable in meaning, and in such cases (e.g. *Arber, Knot, Numbles*) I have given what I believe was his final interpretation. References to *Sir Gawain* (G) and *Pearl* (P) are by stanza, and to *Sir Orfeo* (O) by line.

Arber	Paunch, first stomach of ruminants, G 53.
Assay	The testing of the fat of a deer, and the proper point at which to make the test, G 53.
Assoiled	Absolved, G 75.
Baldric	A belt passing over one shoulder and under the other, supporting a sword or a horn, G 100, 101; a strap to suspend the shield, G 27.
Barbican	A strong outer defence of a castle, over a bridge or gate, connected with the main work, G 34.
Barrow	Mound, G 87.

Beaver	Moveable front part of a helmet, protecting the face, G 26.
Blazon	Shield, G 27, 35.
Blear	Dim, P 7.
Brawn	Flesh, G 64, 65.
Buffet	Blow, G 94.
Caitiff	Boor, one of base mind and conduct, G 71.
Capadoce	*This word is taken from the original; it apparently meant* a short cape, that could be buttoned or clasped round the throat, G 9, 25.
Caparison	Ornamented cloth covering of a horse, G 26.
Carl	Man, G 84.
Carols	Dances accompanied by song, G 3; cf. *carol dances*, G 66, 75, and *they carolled*, G 42.
Childermas	The feast of the Holy Innocents, on the 28th of December, G 42.
Chine	Backbone, G 54.
Churl	Common man, G 84.
Cincture	Girdle, G 98.
Cithern	Stringed instrument, P 8.
Coat-armour	Surcoat worn over the armour, embroidered with distinctive heraldic devices, G 25, 81.
Cognisance	*literally* 'recognition', i.e. a personal badge by which the wearer could be known (referring to the Pentangle), G 81.
Coif	Head-dress, G 69.
Corses	Bodies, P 72.
Crenelles	Battlements, G 34 (*strictly*, the indentations in the battlements, alternating with the raised parts, the 'merlons').
Crupper	Leather strap passing round a horse's hind-quarters and fastened to the saddle to prevent it from slipping forward, G 8, 26.

Cuisses	Armour for the thighs, G 25.
Demeaned her	Behaved, G 51.
Dolour	Sorrow, P 28.
Doted	Gone out of their wits, G 78.
Ellwand	Measuring-rod an ell (45 inches) long, G 10.
Empery	Absolute dominion, P 38.
Eslot	Hollow above the breastbone at the base of the throat, G 53; = *neck-slot*, G 63.
Fain	Glad, G 35.
Featly	Neatly, G 34; deftly, skilfully, G 51.
Feigned	Formed, fashioned, P 63.
Fells	Skins, G 37, 69; *fox-fell*, G 77.
Finials	Ornamental pinnacles on rooves or towers, G 34.
Flower-de-luce	iris (*in the translation specifically* a white iris), P 17, 63.
Fore-numbles	*The original has 'avanters', part of the numbles of a deer, see Numbles;* G 53.
Frore	Very cold, frosty, P 90.
Gittern	Stringed instrument, P 8.
Glair	White of egg, P 86.
Glamoury	Enchantment (enchanted being), G 99.
Gledes	Live coals, G 64.
Gramercy	Thank you, G 35, 42, 85.
Greaves	Armour for the legs, G 25.
Greet	Weep, O 104.
Grue	Shuddering horror, G 95.
Guerdon	Reward, recompense, G 72, 82; P 51, 52.
Guisarm	Battle-axe, G 13, 15, 17, 91.
Gules	Heraldic name for red, G 27, 28.
Halidom	*In the oath 'So help me God and the Halidom', 'the Halidom' referred to* something of

	reverence or sanctity on which the oath was taken; G 85.
Handsels	Gifts at New Year, G 4.
Hap	Fortune, P 11.
Hastlets	Edible entrails of a pig, G 64.
Heathenesse	The heathen lands, O 513.
Hie	Hasten, G 53.
Holt	Wood, G 68,
Ingle	Fire burning on the hearth, G 66.
Keep	(*probably*) guard, protect, O 233.
Kerchiefs	Head-coverings, G 39.
Kirtle	A short coat or tunic reaching to the knees, G 73, P 17.
Knot	*Technical term applied to* two pieces of fat in the neck and two in the flanks, G 53.
Latchet	Loop, lace, fastening, G 26.
Lemman	Lover, mistress, G 71.
Liever	Rather, G 50, O 177.
Link-men	Torch-carriers, G 79.
List	Wished, G 61.
Loopholes	Narrow slits in a castle-wall, G 34.
Ma fay!	By my faith! G 59.
Marge	Edge, G 87.
Margery-pearls	pearls, P 17.
Margery-stones	pearls, P 18.
Maugre	In spite of; *maugre his teeth*, in spite of all he could do to resist, G 62.
Meed	Reward, P 47.
Mellay	Close hand-to-hand combat, G 63.
Molains	Ornamented bosses on a horse's bit, G 8.
Numbles	Pieces of loin-meat, *probably* the tenderloin or fillet, G 53.
Oratory	Chapel, G 88.

Palfrey	Small saddle-horse (especially for the use of women), o 156.
Pauncer	Armour protecting the abdomen, G 80.
Pease	Pea, G 95.
Pisane	Armour for upper breast and neck, G 10.
Pleasances	Pleasure gardens, P 12.
Point-device	To perfection, G 26.
Poitrel	Breast-armour of a horse, G 8, 26.
Polains	Pieces of armour for the knees, G 25.
Popinjays	Parrots, G 26.
Port	Bearing, G 39.
Prise	*literally* capture, taking, G 64; notes blown on the horn at the taking or felling of the hunted beast, G 54.
Purfling	Embroidered border, P 18.
Quadrate	Square, P 87.
Quarry	Heap of slain animals, P 53.
Quest	Searching of hounds after game; *cried for a quest*, called for a search (by baying), G 57.
Rewel	Some kind of ivory, P 18.
Rood	Cross, P 54, 59, 68.
Ruth	Remorse, G 100.
Sabatons	Steel shoes, G 25.
Sendal	A fine silken material, G 4.
Sheen	Bright, P 4.
Slade	Valley, P 12.
Surnape	Napkin, *or* overcloth to protect tablecloth, G 37.
Tables	Horizontal courses, the stepped tiers of the foundation, P 83.
Tabour	Small drum, o 301.
Tabourers	Players on the tabour, o 521.
Tenoned	Closely joined, P 83.

Tines	Pointed branches of a deer's horn, G 34.
Tors	High hills, P 73.
Tressure	Jewelled net confining the hair, G 69.
Vair	Variegated (grey and white) squirrel's fur, O 241.
Weasand	Oesophagus, gullet, G 53.
Weed	Garment, G 95; *weeds*, P 64, O 146.
Welkin	Heavens, sky, G 23, P 10.
Wight	Being, G 84.
Wist	Knew, G 61.
Worms	Dragons, serpents, G 31.
Wrack	Drifting cloud, G 68.

APPENDIX

The Verse-forms of
Sir Gawain and the Green Knight
and *Pearl*

I SIR GAWAIN

The word 'alliterative', as applied to the ancestral measure of England, is misleading; for it was not concerned with *letters*, with *spelling*, but with *sounds*, judged by the ear. The sounds that are important are those that *begin* words – more precisely, those that begin the stressed syllables of words. Alliteration, or 'head-rhyme', is the agreement of stressed syllables within the line in beginning with the same consonantal sound (sound, not letter), or in beginning not with a consonant but with a vowel. Any vowel alliterates with any other vowel: the alliterative pattern is satisfied if the words in question do *not* begin with a consonant.

'Apt alliteration's artful aid,' said an eighteenth-century writer. But to a fourteenth-century poet in this mode three only of those four words alliterated. Not *alliteration* itself; for its first strong syllable is *lit*, and so it alliterates on the consonant *l*. *Apt*, *artful*, and *aid* alliterate; not because they begin with the same *letter*, *a*, but because they agree in beginning with no consonant; and that was alliteration enough. 'Old English art', where the words begin with three different letters, would be just as good.

But a line of this verse was not verse simply because it contained such alliterations; *rum ram ruf*, as Chaucer's parson mocked it, is not a line. It also had some structure.

The poet begins his poem with a very regular line, of one of his favourite varieties:

> Siþen þe sege and þe assaut watz sesed at Troye
> When the siege and the assault had ceased at Troy

This kind of line falls into two parts: 'When the siege and the assault' and 'had ceased at Troy.' There is nearly always a breath-pause between them, corresponding to some degree of pause in the sense. But the line was welded into a metrical unit by alliteration; one or more (usually two) of the chief words in the first part were linked by alliteration with the *first* important word in the second part. Thus, in the line above, *siege, assault; ceased*. (As it is the stressed syllable that counts, *assault* runs on *s*, not on a vowel).

Each of these parts had to contain two syllables (often whole words, like *siege*) that were in their place sufficiently stressed to bear a 'beat'. The other syllables should be lighter and quieter. But their number was not counted, nor in this medieval form was their placing strictly ordered. This freedom has one marked effect on rhythm: there might be no intervening light syllable between the stresses. It is of course an effect far easier to produce in English than to avoid, being normal in natural speech. Verse that uses it can accommodate easily many natural phrasings. The medieval poets used it especially in the second part of their lines; examples from the translation are

Tirius went to Tuscany   and tówns fóunded   (stanza 1)
Indeed of the Table Round   all those tríed bréthren   (stanza 3)

The alliteration may be at a minimum, affecting only one word in each part of the line. This is not frequent in the original (and in some places of its occurrence mistakes in the manuscript may be suspected); it is somewhat more so in the translation. Far more often, the alliteration is increased. Mere excess, when both of the stresses in the second part alliterate, is seldom found; two examples occur in consecutive lines in stanza 83:

> þay *bo3*en bi *b*onkkez   þer *bo3*es are *b*are,
>
> þay *c*lomben bi *c*lyffez   þer *c*lengez þe *c*olde

and are preserved in the translation. This is an excess, a rum-ram-ruf-*ram*, that soon cloys the ear.

Increased alliteration is usually connected with increase in weight and content of the line. In very many verses the first part of the line has three heavy syllables or beats (not necessarily, nor indeed usually, of equal force). It is convenient to look at this sort of rhythm in this way. Natural language does not always arrange itself into the simple patterns:

> the siege and the assault   had ceased at Troy
>
> Tirius to Tuscany   and towns founded

There might be more 'full words' in a phrase. 'The king and his kinsman/and courtly men served them.' (see stanza 21, line 16) is well enough and is a sufficient line. But you might wish to say: 'The king and his good kinsman/and quickly courtly men served them.' As far as the second half of the line went, you restrained your wish and did not allow the language to have its head; you kept the ends of lines simple and clear. At most you would venture on 'and courtiers at once served them' – avoiding double alliteration and putting the adverb where in natural narration it could be subordinated in force and tone to *court-* and *served*, leaving them plainly as the beats. But in the first part of the line 'packing' was much practiced.

In 'The king and his good kinsman' *good* is not of much importance, and can be reduced in tone so as hardly to rise up and challenge the main beats, *king* and *kin*. But if this element joins in the alliteration, it is brought into notice, and then one has a triple type: 'The king and his kind kinsman'. This variety, in which there is a third beat inserted before the second main beat, to which it is subordinated in tone and import, but with which it nonetheless alliterates, is very common indeed. Thus the second line of the poem:

And the *f*ortress *f*ell in *f*lame   to *f*irebrands and ashes

But the added material may come at the beginning of the line. Instead of 'In pomp and pride/he peopled it first' (see the 9th line of the poem) you may say: 'In great pomp and pride'. This will lead easily to another variety in which there is a third beat before the first main stress, to which it is subordinate, but with which it alliterates; so in the eighth line of the poem:

Fro *r*iche *R*omulus to *R*ome   *r*icchis hym swyþe
When *r*oyal *R*omulus to *R*ome his   *r*oad had taken

Less commonly a full but subordinate word may be put instead of a weak syllable at the end of the first part of the line; thus in stanza 81:

Þe gordel of þe grene silke,   þat gay wel bisemed
That girdle of green silk,   and gallant it looked

If this is given an alliteration, one gets the type:

And *f*ar over the *F*rench *f*lood   *F*elix Brutus   (stanza 1)

Further varieties will then develop; for example, those in which the third beat is not really subordinate, but either phonetically, or in sense and vividness, or in both, a rival to the others:

But *w*ild *w*eathers of the *w*orld, a*w*ake in the land
The *r*ings *r*id of the *r*ust   on his *r*ich byrnie   (both from
    stanza 80)

It may sometimes occur that the added beat bears the alliteration and the phonetically or logically more important word does not. In the translation, this type is used in order to provide an alliteration when a main word that cannot be changed refuses to alliterate. Thus in the first line of stanza 2 the translation has:

And when *f*air Britain was *f*ounded   by this *f*amous lord
for the original

Ande quen þis *B*retayn watz *b*igged   bi þis *b*urn rych(e) –

since 'Britain' was inescapable, but neither *bigged* (founded) nor *burn* (knight, man) have any modern counterparts to alliterate with it.

As was said earlier, alliteration was by ear, and not by letter; the spelling is not concerned.

Ʒusted ful jolilé   þise gentyle kniʒtes   (stanza 3, line 6)

alliterated, despite the spelling with *g* and *j*. Quite another matter is 'licence'. The poet allowed himself certain of these: where neither the spelling nor the sound were the same, but the sounds were at least *similar*. He could occasionally disregard the distinction between voiced and voiceless consonants, and thus equate *s* with *z*, or *f* with *v*, and (often) words beginning with *h* with words beginning with a vowel. In the translation the same licences are allowed when necessary – a translator needs even more help than one composing on his own.
Thus:

Quen Zeferus syflez hymself   on sedez and erbez
When Zephyr goes sighing   through seeds and herbs
   (stanza 23)

and:

Though you yourself be desirous   to accept it in person
   (stanza 16)

where the second stress is the 'zire' of *desirous*, and the third is the 'sept' of *accept*.

The cases where the alliteration is borne not by the first but by the second element in a compound word (such as *eye-lid* or *daylight* in lines alliterating on *l*) are really not different metrically from those in which a separate but subordinate word usurps the alliteration. For example:

And unlouked his yʒe-lyddez,   and let as him wondered
He lifted his eyelids   with a look as of wonder   (stanza 48)

One variety is frequently used in the translation which is not often found in clear cases in the original; that is 'crossed alliteration'. In this, a line contains two alliterative sounds, in either the arrangement *abab* or *abba*. These patterns are used in the translation because they satisfy the requirements of simple alliteration and yet add more metrical colour to make up for the cases where triple or quadruple alliteration in the original cannot be rivalled in modern English. Thus:

All of *g*reen were they *m*ade,   both *g*arments and *m*an
  (stanza 8)

Towards the *f*airest at the *t*able   he *t*wisted the *f*ace
  (stanza 20)

In the following line the pattern is ʃ/s/ʒ/ʃ:

And since *f*olly thou hast sought,   thou deservest to *f*ind it
  (stanza 15)

The frequent occurrence in the translation of 'Wawain' for 'Gawain' follows the practice of the original. Both forms of the name were current; and of course the existence of an alternative form of the name of a principal character, beginning with another consonant, was a great help to an alliterative poet.

But in *Sir Gawain* there is end-rhyme as well, in the last lines of each stanza. The author had the notion (so it may probably be said, for nothing quite like it is found elsewhere) to lighten the monotony and weight of some 2,000 long alliterating lines on end. He broke them up into groups (hardly really 'stanzas', as they are very variable in length), and at the end of each he put a patch of rhyme. This consists of four three-beat lines rhyming alternative (now known as the 'wheel') and a one-beat tag (known as the 'bob') to link the 'wheel' with the preceding stanza. The bob rhymes with the second and fourth lines of the wheel. There is no doubt of the metrical success of this device; but since the rhymed lines had also to alliterate, and there is not much room to move in the short lines of the wheel, the author set himself a severe technical test, and the translator a worse one. In the translation, the attempt to alliterate as well as rhyme has had to be abandoned a little more often than in the original. As an example of the bob and wheel both in the original and in the translation, this is the end of stanza 2:

> If ze wyl lysten þis laye bot on littel quile
> I schal telle hit astit, as I in toun herde,
>> with tonge,
>> As hit is stad and stoken
>> In stori stif and stronge,
>> With lei letteres loken,
>> In londe so hatz ben longe.
> If you will listen to this lay but a little while now,
> I will tell it at once as in town I have heard
>> it told,
>> as it is fixed and fettered
>> in story brave and bold,
>> thus linked and truly lettered
>> as was loved in this land of old.

II PEARL

In *Pearl* the author adopted a twelve-line rhyming stanza in which alliteration is used as well. The line in *Pearl* is a French line, modified primarily (a) by the difference of English from French generally, and (b) by the influence of inherited metrical practices and taste, especially in the areas where the alliterative tradition was still strong. The essential features of the ancient English alliterative practice are wholly unlike, in effect and aim, what is found in *Pearl*. In the old alliterative verse the 'line' had no repeated or constant accentual rhythm which gave it its metrical character; its units were the half-lines, each of which was independently constructed. The line was internally linked by alliteration; but this linking was deliberately used *counter* to the rhetorical and syntactic structure. The chief rhetorical or logical pauses were normally placed (except at the end of a verse period of several lines) in the middle of the line between the alliterations; and the second half-line was most frequently more closely connected in sense and syntax to the following line.

In complete contrast to all this, there is in *Pearl* a basic and model accentual rhythm of alternating strong/loud – weak/soft syllables; the poem being written to a scheme:

x / x / x / x / (x)

þay songen wyth a swete asent   (line 94 of the original).

'Model' lines of this kind make up about a quarter of the lines in the poem; but if those lines are included in which there occurs the simple variation of allowing one of the 'falls' to contain *two* weak syllables, the proportion rises to about three-fifths, and higher still if two such two-syllable falls are allowed. In all these cases (since only those in which the metrically unstressed elements are genuinely 'weak' are counted) the metrical pattern of alternating strong-loud and weak-soft syllables is clearly maintained. And in spite of the 'variations' that are used, and of the doubt concerning the presence or absence of final -*e*, this pattern remains indeed so frequent and insistent as to impart to the metrical effect of the whole a certain monotony, which combined with the emphasis of alliteration can (at any rate to a modern listener) become almost soporific. This is increased by the poet's preference for making the last beat, which is a rhyming syllable, share in the alliteration.

In *Pearl* the *total line* is the unit, and is usually 'locked up in itself'; in the vast majority of cases, the major marks of punctuation must be placed at the line-ends. Even 'commas', when phonetically used (that is, when not used simply by custom, to mark off phrases which are not naturally marked off even by light pauses in speech) are infrequent within the line; while 'run-ons' from one line to the next are extremely rare.

And finally, alliteration in the verse-form of *Pearl* plays *no* structural part in the line at all. It may be divided among the four stresses in any order or amount from two to four, and where there is only one pair these may be placed together as AB or as CD, leaving the other half alliteratively blank. And it may be absent altogether; in the 1,212 lines of the poem, over 300 are quite blank. Moreover, unless the number of blank lines is to be made even larger, syllables may assist in alliteration that do not bear the main metrical stresses, or are in the structure of the line relatively weak. In other words, alliteration is in *Pearl* a mere 'grace' or decoration of the line, which is sufficiently defined as such, and as being 'verse', without it. And this decoration is provided according to the skill of the poet, or linguistic opportunity, without guiding rule or other function.

Each stanza of *Pearl* has twelve lines, containing only three rhymes, always arranged *ab* in the first eight and then *bcbc* in the last four. The whole poem would contain 100 stanzas in twenty groups of five, if the fifteenth group (which begins with stanza 71) did not contain six. It has been argued that a stanza has been included in the manuscript which the author meant to strike out; but against this is the fact that the extra stanza in *Pearl* gives the poem a total of 101, and there are 101 stanzas in *Sir Gawain*.

The groups of five stanzas (which are indicated in the manuscript by an ornamental coloured initial at the beginning of each group) are constituted in this way. The last word in each stanza reappears in the first line of the following one (so stanza 1 ends in the original Of þat pryuy perle wythouten *spot*', and stanza 2 begins 'Syþen in þat *spote* hit fro me sprange'). This link-word reappears in the first line of the first stanza of the following group (so stanza 6 begins 'Fro *spot* my spyryt þer sprang in space'), and the new link-word appears at the end of that stanza (so stanza 6 ends 'Of half so dere adubbemente', and stanza 7 begins 'Dubbed wern alle þo downez sydez'). As this last instance shows, the link need not be precisely the same, but may be constituted from different parts of the same verb, from noun and adjective with the same stem, and so on. The linkage fails in the original at the beginning of stanza 61, as it does in the translation.

Thus not only are the stanzas linked together internally as groups, but the groups are linked to each other; and the last line of the poem, 'And precious perlez vnto his pay' (where *pay* means 'pleasure') echoes the first, 'Perle, plesaunte to prynces paye.' This echoing of the beginning of the poem in its end is found also in *Sir Gawain*, and in *Patience*.

This form was not easy to compose in, but very much more difficult to translate in; since the rhyme-words used by the poet rarely still fit in modern English, and the alliterating words fit as seldom. In the translation, satisfaction of the rhyme-scheme is of course given the primacy, and the alliteration is less rich than in the original. But the effect of the translation on the modern ear is probably that of its original on a contemporary ear in this respect, since we no longer habitually expect alliteration as an essential ingredient in verse, as the people of the North and West of England once did.

GAWAIN'S LEAVE-TAKING

Now Lords and Ladies blithe and bold,
      To bless you here now am I bound:
I thank you all a thousand-fold,
    And pray God save you whole and sound;
    Wherever you go on grass or ground,
        May he you guide that nought you grieve,
    For friendship that I here have found
        Against my will I take my leave.

For friendship and for favours good,
    For meat and drink you heaped on me,
The Lord that raised was on the Rood
    Now keep you comely company.
    On sea or land where'er you be,
        May he you guide that nought you grieve,
    Such fair delight you laid on me
        Against my will I take my leave.

Against my will although I wend,
    I may not always tarry here;
For everything must have an end,
    And even friends must part, I fear;
    Be we beloved however dear
        Out of this world death will us reave,
    And when we brought are to our bier
        Against our will we take our leave.

Now good day to you, goodmen all,
    And good day to you, young and old,
And good day to you, great and small,
    And gramercy a thousand-fold!
    If ought there were that dear ye hold,
        Full fain I would the deed achieve –
    Now Christ you keep from sorrows cold
        For now at last I take my leave.